The Care and Keeping of Freddy

Also by Susan Hill Long

Josie Bloom and the Emergency of Life

The Care and Keeping of Freddy

Susan Hill Long

A Paula Wiseman Book

Simon & Schuster Books for Young Readers

NEW YORK   LONDON   TORONTO   SYDNEY   NEW DELHI

SIMON & SCHUSTER BOOKS FOR YOUNG READERS

An imprint of Simon & Schuster Children's Publishing Division

1230 Avenue of the Americas, New York, New York 10020

SIMON & SCHUSTER BOOKS FOR YOUNG READERS

and related marks are trademarks of Simon & Schuster, Inc.

For information about special discounts for bulk purchases, please contact Simon & Schuster Special Sales at 1-866-506-1949 or business@simonandschuster.com.

The Simon & Schuster Speakers Bureau can bring authors to your live event. For more information or to book an event, contact the Simon & Schuster Speakers Bureau at 1-866-248-3049 or visit our website at www.simonspeakers.com.

Interior design by Hilary Zarycky

The text for this book was set in Bodoni Twelve ITC.

Manufactured in the United States of America

0821 FFG

First Edition

2 4 6 8 10 9 7 5 3 1

Library of Congress Cataloging-in-Publication Data

Names: Long, Susan Hill, 1965- author.

Title: The care and keeping of Freddy / Susan Long.

Description: First edition. | New York : Simon & Schuster Books for Young Readers, [2021] | "A Paula Wiseman Book." | Audience: Ages 8-12. | Audience: Grades 4-6. | Summary: Friends Georgia, Maria, and Roly stumble through a pivotal summer together as parents, siblings, and a bearded dragon named Freddy cause distress.

Identifiers: LCCN 2020056789 | ISBN 9781534475199 (hardcover) ISBN 9781534475212 (ebook)

Subjects: CYAC: Friendship–Fiction. | Family life–Maine–Fiction. | Bearded dragons (Reptiles) as pets–Fiction. | Maine–Fiction.

Classification: LCC PZ7.L8582 Car 2021 | DDC [Fic]–dc23

LC record available at https://lccn.loc.gov/2020056789

For Matt, again
—S.H.L.

Chapter 1

Give Freddy a Better Life."

It was January when Georgia Weathers wrote that note and taped it to the side of Freddy's tank. Now, somehow, it was June. The ink had faded, the paper had curled. Freddy's life was not better. And if Patty van Winkle just said what Georgia *thought* she said, then things were about to get worse.

Georgia's best friend, Maria Elena Garcia, stood beside her at the Pet Stop pet shop. Maria lifted her eyebrows, poked up her glasses, and frowned around the pen between her teeth.

Georgia swallowed hard. "Did you say . . . hissing . . . cockroaches?"

"*Ay Dios mío*," Maria muttered as she pushed aside

a lock of black hair that dropped as if in shock across her cheek. Maria's family was from Mexico, on her father's side. Her mother was from Mexico, too—the town of Mexico, Maine! Maria liked to copy her grandmother's dramatic expressions when circumstances called for them.

"Correct!" said Patty van Winkle. "There's a tri-state shortage of crickets."

Maria popped the pen from her mouth, flicked her hair back, and flipped open a small, spiral-bound notebook. "Innnteresting," she muttered. "Definitely jot-worthy." Maria declared many things interesting and jot-worthy. Many things caused Maria's dark eyes to sharpen behind the pink plastic frames of her eyeglasses. She longed to be a writer of romance, or possibly suspense.

"Don't you worry, Georgia," Patty van Winkle said. "Bearded dragons aren't as picky as you'd think. Freddy will gobble 'em right up. No problem. Right as rain. A bug's a bug."

Georgia felt a bobble in her chest. It felt—*gulp*—like a bug. Why was it that cockroaches seemed infinitely worse than crickets? And hissing cockroaches seemed much worse than regular, non-hissing ones. "I have to think about the . . . the nutritional alternative."

"All righty, then." Patty put a box of what were almost certainly cockroaches onto the counter as if Georgia didn't have any choice about buying them, which, she supposed, she didn't. "You'll see," Patty said, "cockroaches will suit Freddy's reptilian palate. They'll warm his cold-blooded heart."

Blythe—Georgia's mother—had always been fond of surprises. The day Georgia got Freddy, Patty van Winkle had accepted delivery of a bearded dragon by mistake. "The Pet Stop does not handle this sort of unique, one-of-a-kind exotic creature," Patty told Georgia's mother that day. They all three stared at the baby lizard, with his warty hide and a jagged edge of spines along his throat. "I'll be shipping him back, pronto."

"Oh no you will not, Patty van Winkle." Georgia's mother had knelt before Georgia in the pet shop. Blonde curled hair fell shining to her shoulders. Her coral-pink lipstick had gotten onto her teeth, which Georgia could plainly see because of how her mother was smiling in a big way that made Georgia feel strange in her stomach, as if she'd swallowed an ice cube whole. Blythe's cotton dress was crisp and pretty under her pink cardigan sweater, and it had little buttons all up and down the front, from the collar to the hem above the knee. "I am determined to purchase this exotic creature for my daughter," her mother had said, "to have and to hold."

"She ain't gonna marry it, Blythe," said Patty.

Blythe smiled, cupping Georgia's chin. "This lizard represents my love for you."

"Cold-blooded?" said Patty.

Blythe stared straight into Georgia's eyes. "Undying," she said.

"Says here"—Patty was scanning a pamphlet marked *The Care and Keeping of Your Bearded Dragon*—"they live eight to fifteen years in captivity. What do you suppose happens after *that*?"

Blythe's eyes narrowed, and she sliced a glare at Patty. "Eight years, fifteen years—who cares? It's a lifetime." She turned back to Georgia. "It's forever." Then she kissed Georgia's cheeks, *smack-smack*, and stood up. "Georgia," she said, "you will remember this day."

Georgia remembered, all right. That was the day Blythe left town with Lyle Lenczycki.

Now a clacking, shifting, scrabbling noise came from the cardboard box. A noise like pebbles shifting underfoot, pulled by a wave at the beach. Georgia sighed, although Blythe had always frowned on sighing: "You sound like a little old lady at all of eight and a half." Georgia was eleven now, and had gone on to sigh many times. Sighing cooled her internal worry machine.

Hissing cockroaches. Freddy's life was definitely worse.

Chapter 2

Just then the little bell jingled above the door. Georgia and Maria whipped around to look at the door and the boy coming in it. He was about Georgia's age. He had red hair and blue eyes and his ears stuck out; the tips of them were sunburned. He wore baggy shorts and mismatched socks and brand-new white sneakers with rubber toe bumpers, and his T-shirt was printed with a message: KEEP ON TRUCKIN'. Georgia had never seen him in her life. Maria's eyebrows shot up under blunt-cut bangs. She poked the bridge of her glasses and started jotting. Patty smiled encouragingly from her side of the counter.

"Welcome to the Pet Stop, Mr. . . . uh . . . "

The boy glanced at Georgia and Maria. "They sent me for boat food."

Patty repeated it. "Boat food."

"That's what I said." The boy jammed his fists in the pockets of his shorts and hunched his shoulders up near the stick-out ears.

Maria was still writing. The point of her tongue poked out from the corner of her mouth, and her black hair was starting to frizz a little, what with all the humidity and excitement in the air. Everybody knew everybody in Prospect Harbor, Maine; it was seldom that a stranger came to town.

Georgia stuffed her fists into the front pockets of her shorts. Then she yanked them out again, in case it seemed like she'd copied the boy. She wished she could think of something original to do with her hands.

"Boat!" burst forth from Patty van Winkle. "You're here for *Boat's* food. Boat is Winslow Farley's betta," she said. "His fish. That must make you the Farleys' new kid. Roland, right? Roland Park?"

Roland Park nodded one time. Chin down, chin up.

"Well, you've come to the right place," Patty went on. "I'm just unboxing stock. Give me a sec—I have to grab it from the back." She disappeared into the back room.

Now the pet shop was quiet, except for the sounds of a couple guinea pigs rustling around in their pine shavings and the *click-a-click* of Maria's pen. Georgia tried to think of something to say. Eventually she cleared her throat. The boy stared at her. "I'm here for the cockroaches," Georgia said loudly. Maria glanced up from her notebook and gave Georgia a pitying look.

The boy glided more than walked—a slippery sort of move—to a spinner rack of leashes and collars. He plucked a thin little cat collar off the rack and slipped it into his pocket, all in the blink of an eye. Georgia wasn't even sure of what she'd seen. Had that boy just stolen a cat collar? Maria had seen it, too—her eyes were open wide, and so was her mouth. She was about to yell; Maria was not afraid of yelling. And then, for some reason she couldn't say, Georgia shot out her hand and clapped it over Maria's mouth.

They were frozen that way—the boy with his hands in his pockets, Maria's eyes bulging, Georgia's hand covering Maria's mouth—when Patty van Winkle returned carrying a shaker of fish food. Patty's eyes narrowed. It wasn't for nothing that her ex was a police officer, as Patty had said more than once.

Georgia said, "Maria here was going to cough." Maria obliged: *Cuh-cuh.* Georgia leveled a look at her, and then lowered her hand.

"Gerrrms," said Maria. "Baaad." Then she wrote something in her notebook.

Patty nodded as if all that seemed perfectly normal, and the boy, Roland Park, gave her the money and took the bag with the fish food and walked out the door without even a thank-you. The bell above the door made a cheerful *jing-a-ling*, which Georgia found unsuitable, considering a crime had just been committed. Maria went after him.

Georgia paid for Freddy's box of cockroaches and hustled out the door.

Chapter 3

Most of the municipal buildings of Prospect Harbor—the library, town hall, fire station, post office—bordered the four sides of the town green at irregular intervals, like hotels on a Monopoly board in early rounds of the game. The Pet Stop, too, was situated on the green, on the north side; Patty's business had taken over the old pool hall when people decided pets were more important than pool in terms of prime real estate.

Outside the Pet Stop now, Maria was scribbling and stumbling after Roland. Also yelling. "Hey, you!"

Roland picked up his pace. He was cutting south across the green.

"Roland?" Georgia yelled. She didn't yell as forcibly

as Maria—she wasn't nearly as practiced at yelling—but she did add the personal touch of his name. "We saw you," she said. "We *see* you," she called, this time a little louder. Roland stopped and turned around. Maria clicked her pen like crazy.

Roland strolled back to them, lazily swinging the bag with the fish food—so lazily it appeared to be a lot of work. "Yeah?" he said. "Just what do you think you saw?"

Maria adjusted her eyeglasses, cleared her throat—*ah-hem*—and proceeded to read from her notebook. "Subject: Boy, aged approximately ten—"

"Twelve!"

"Noted...," Maria said, with the slightest tilt of her head. "Tall as a small *tree*; handsome as a *movie star*, eyes *blue sapphires* in a face as white as *snow*; teeth as straight and even as a *picket fence*; copper hair shining like the moonlit, storm-tossed *waters of the sea*." She smiled at Roland.

Wow. Georgia blushed on Maria's behalf.

Roland's mouth was hanging open, and so Georgia studied what she could see of his teeth. Actually, they were not that straight.

Maria continued to read. "Subject crosses to spinner rack. Pilfers pink, rhinestone-studded cat collar.

Stuffs in right front pocket of shorts." Maria looked up from the page. "I taught myself shorthand over winter vacation," she said, and lowered her lids modestly.

Roland, staring, ran a hand over his head, maybe to see if it felt storm-tossed or moonlit. Then he shook himself, and finally blinked. "It wasn't *pink*."

Maria tucked her frizzing hair behind her ear. "It is the job of a writer to put the pizzazz on the page," she said.

Roland blinked again.

"Now." Maria flipped to a new sheet. "How about you tell us *what* you're doing here and where you come from and how long you're staying and why?"

Roland dropped the Pet Stop bag on the ground and crossed his arms. "Yeah, okay, how about you write this down for the record? My parents are the president and first lady of the United States of Blah-blah, and I am here on a mission to bring the outside world to this stupid, Podunk, one-light—make that one-*stop-sign*—town, and I'm staying for as short a time as humanly possible, because"—he gulped—"because somebody"—his eyes darted as if he was searching for the next thing to say—"because somebody *important* is coming to get me." Roland puffed out his chest and tilted up his chin and looked right down his nose like he thought he was an important person. Or maybe because he *didn't*.

Georgia often acted the opposite of how she felt. For example, she'd found that if you whistle, people figure you haven't got a care in the world. "*Some*one's happy," they'll say, when maybe you're not happy at all. Maybe you're sad, or confused, or feeling alone in a crowd. Sometimes you have a feeling, but you're not sure what it is. Whistling gives a person time to think.

But this was no time for whistling. Georgia was determined, at that moment, to think something, to feel something, and to act. She was kind of mad at that boy Roland Park for shoplifting that cat collar and for being generally unfriendly when *they* were all being especially *nice*, because of him being a stranger, a new boy. And she had surprised herself, back in the store—the not telling, the letting him walk away. The aiding and abetting, as Maria might put it, maybe *did* put it, in her notebook.

The box of cockroaches rattled. "We didn't tell on you," Georgia said. "You should at least tell us—" *Tell us what?* "You should tell us something real."

Roland Park stared at her. Then he looked sideways and made a long *pffffffff* sound. He shoved his fists in his pockets again and looked at the sky and bunched up his shoulders and let them drop. "If you have to know, my dad's *incarcerated*, and they declared my mom *unfit* due to one thing and another, and so they put me in the system."

"What's the system?" said Maria.

"Who's *they*?" said Georgia.

"The foster care system. The Farleys are my foster parents. Winslow is my foster brother. Winslow's pet fish is my foster pet fish. Get it?"

Maria shook out her writing hand. "Cute kid, you could've done worse."

"Believe me, it's all temporary. I got a *real* brother—"

"Who's *they*?" Georgia said again. She really wanted to know who, exactly, was making all the big decisions in life. "You said *they*."

Roland shrugged. "They. Them. Those ones. I got dumped here on Saturday," Roland went on. "Dumped like a bag of rocks, and then we spent all of Sunday at church."

"Holy Redeemer?" Maria wanted to know.

"Voice of the Trumpet."

Maria jotted.

"You get all that?" Roland jutted his chin at Maria and her notebook and pen.

"Absolutely." Maria was sweating. The brown skin of her knuckles had gone white from gripping the pen. She clicked it. "Now, where'd you live before? Did they kick you out? How long will you live here? Do you wish—"

Roland shot his hands in the air. "Enough already!" he said, then landed them on top of his head. "Geez Loise!"

Maria shrugged, then smiled. "I've got all the time in the world to write a character study of Roland Park," she said.

Roland dug one white-sneakered heel and then the other into the dirt "Well, I better get this fish food over to Boat," he said, bending to pick up the bag. "Thanks for not telling. You two are all right." Then he started walking away.

Georgia watched him with a feeling of disappointment. She had thought he would go back in there and put the cat collar back, if given the chance. But there he was, starting again across the green. "Where are you going?" Georgia called out.

"I just *said*," Roland shot over his shoulder.

"Aren't you going to put that collar back?" Georgia wondered why she'd believed he would. It wasn't as if people always did what you'd counted on them to do.

Maria pushed up her sliding glasses. "Every character must have a defining feature," she shouted. "Do you want yours to be"—she read from her notebook—"sneaky, untrustworthy, treacherous, and disloyal?"

There passed a long, long moment during which Roland stopped on the path, turned, and narrowed his eyes first at Maria, then at Georgia. Apparently he had to think about it. "That's more than one defining feature," he finally said.

"But we didn't tell on you." Georgia thought of the thing her father sometimes said—he'd said it just last night over the checkerboard—when he wanted her to reconsider a move. Sometimes, it seemed like he wasn't talking about chess or checkers. It seemed like he was talking about *Life*. So she said the thing. "Roland Park," she said, "don't you wish you could make the better move?"

She hoped she was offering Roland a chance to think things over. "You *can*, if you want to," she added. Roland was standing there, scowling. But the important thing was the standing-there part. He hadn't walked away. He hadn't left. So she did what seemed to her a very grown-up thing to do: She stuck out her hand to Roland Park. "Shake on it?" she said.

Roland looked at Georgia's hand like he might spit on it. "You know, I was starting to think that for the short and miserable time I gotta stick around here, you two would be my *friends*. You know, *real* friends. People who'd lie for you."

Maria's pen shot straight to her notebook. "Innnn-teresting."

Georgia willed herself not to blink, so that when Roland looked her way he would find her staring at him, staring straight into his soul. Her arm was getting tired. She made a bargain with the universe: If he shook on it, they could be friends; if he didn't shake on it, then they couldn't. They wouldn't.

Roland took a few steps closer, turned on one heel, and back again. He kicked the ground, shook his head, mumbled at the sky. He squinted down the path as if figuring the odds of escape. Then he kicked the dirt again, while out of his mouth came sounds like *awwwsh* and *pffffffff*. Georgia's arm was about to fall off. Her hand was still stuck out there in front of her, waiting for him to take it. *Click-a-click*, went Maria's pen. *Click-a-click*.

"Aw heck—and it's *Roly*, not Roland." Roland grabbed Georgia's hand and shook it, up-down. "I *have* to make a couple friends, or else Mrs. Farley'll invite the whole stupid Sunday school for a holy potluck."

Then Roly went back inside the Pet Stop to the tune of Maria's pen scratching and the bell above the door going *jing-a-ling-a-ling*.

Chapter 4

The next day, Georgia and Maria rode their bikes slowly past the Farleys' house on Cross Street. They were on their way to check the mail at the post office, but that didn't mean they had to take the direct route. They rode by the Farleys' place again. They had all day to check the mail. The third time they rode by the house, Roland Park came out of it.

Georgia and Maria hopped off their bikes. A curtain twitched and parted, and the pale, narrow face of little Winslow Farley peered out. Georgia waved. Maria waved. Roland—Roly—did not wave. Georgia and Maria walked their bikes beside him.

"Praise the Lord you rode by." The way he said it, Roly was possibly taking the Lord's name in vain. "I don't know if I can stand another Bible verse," he said.

"Then the Lord commanded the fish!" said Maria. "And it vomited Jonah up onto the dry land."

Roly frowned. "That's not a real Bible verse."

"Yes it is; it's my favorite." Maria smiled a little smile and tilted her head. "How's your cat?"

"What cat?" said Roly.

"*Ex-act-ly*," Maria said as she pulled her bike up short. "Why'd you steal that cat collar, anyway?"

"Well . . . uh, why are *you* wearing a bedspread?" Roly said instead of answering.

Roly was dressed in the same baggy shorts and KEEP ON TRUCKIN' T-shirt as yesterday. Georgia was dressed the same, too. Maria had on a bell-shaped skirt that bunched and gathered around her ankles and threatened to catch in the bike chain. She tugged the bright skirt flat to display the beautiful brocade birds and flowers. "I guess you've never seen a *raboña*?"

Georgia had seen a *raboña*, but only because this was not the first time Maria had worn it. The skirt belonged to Maria's grandmother who lived with them and liked to sigh a lot and say, "I got a cabana at Puerto Escondido calling my name!" whenever things at the Garcias' house got too crazy.

Maria yawned hugely. "Care to know why I just

yawned?" She didn't wait for an answer. "We were up till eleven thirty p.m. playing Hearts around the fire-pit," she said, "till my parents threw us out. Threw us *in*, more like."

The day school let out for the summer, Mr. and Mrs. Garcia moved out of the house and into the old Scamp travel trailer parked behind the garage. Georgia wanted to paint a picture for Roly. "And there are two boys and four girls and one grandmother, and some rabbits, and two dogs." Georgia loved going over to Maria's house. There were colorful things everywhere. There was always somebody talk-talk-talking, or banging on a pots-and-pans drum set, laughing or yelling or even sobbing. There was always plenty going on. Their normal chaos was Georgia's idea of heaven in a house.

"Now Mama and Daddy are out there cooking over an open fire and having a grand old time," said Maria, "while the rest of us are inside changing Maya's diapers, stepping on Marisol's LEGOs, changing *Matilda's* diapers, toiling away over a hot stove . . . I even have a designated apron, for crying out loud. And my *abuela's* no help whatsoever."

"Because of the walker?" said Georgia. Maria's grandma couldn't get around too well.

"Because of she's crabby. She says it's 'cause she quit

smoking again, but guess what? She's still smoking, so what does that tell you?" Maria tugged at the fancy skirt, which had twisted around her knees.

Roly followed this explanation in a sort of stupor, with his mouth open and his eyebrows up past normal.

"Anyway, now they've drawn a perimeter—an imaginary line around the Scamp. If we need something, like Oaty-O's or *toilet* paper, we have to write it on a note and put the note in a bottle and toss the bottle inside the perimeter." Maria shook her head and puffed her bangs up.

A message in a bottle didn't seem all that different from how Georgia talked with her own mom. The distance, the silence. The hollow thing that holds the questions coiled away and stoppered up. Blythe had been gone one year and eight months. Her perimeter was Massachusetts.

Maria puffed her bangs again. "You just sit there on the ground and stare at the bottle," she went on, "wondering if they'll ever come out of the Scamp and get the message or if you're just going to have to eat Cheez Whiz for breakfast again."

Roly snapped to. "I love Cheez Whiz."

"Everybody loves Cheez Whiz, but now my love is ruined."

. . .

Write and wait, wait, wait. Write . . . and . . . wait. Georgia loved getting the letters all the same, *Mrs. Blythe Lenczycki* scribbled in the upper-left corner of the envelope. And the photographs. There was the winter wedding picture: *Lyle* with all that thick dark hair, that porcelain skin, a deep blue band around his middle and a matching bow tie; and Mom looking so pretty in a cream-colored dress and a crown of yellow flowers in her hair. Then came a picture of Blythe with a big belly, filling out the yellow pleats of a maternity dress. And then, last November, came the picture of baby Rosemary.

"One baby sister is great," Maria had told Georgia then, as their heads knocked together over the vision of tiny, bald Rosie and her stretchy pink headband and bow. "Two baby sisters is also pretty good," Maria had said. "Three baby sisters? *Dios mío.*"

Now they'd arrived at the post office. Mr. Grigg hadn't turned around the sign in the window yet; it still said MAIL: NO.

"Might you be expecting a letter, Roly?" Maria said. She was clearly probing for jot-worthy information. "A note from a kindly uncle? A card from Mom or Pop? A package from grandma? What about that brother you mentioned?"

"Nosy," said Roly. He seemed to think about what to say, or *if* to say. "My brother—he's not much for writing."

"Where is he? Do you write him? Your parents?"

"No, I—we don't write each other."

"I can help you write a letter," Maria said. "A letter that'll make him *weep*."

Roly shoved his fists in his pockets and hiked his shoulders. "He's not gonna write," he said, "he's gonna *come* for me."

"Oh?"

"Yeah. Pretty soon, too, he's coming. I don't need a letter, or a call even if I *had* a phone, to know he's coming for me," Roly said louder.

"When, exactly?" Maria was writing everything down. "Are the Farleys aware?"

Roly came up with a date. "August first."

"August first?"

"August first," said Roly, again. "His birthday. The day he turns eighteen."

"Eighteen?"

"That's what I *said*! Drop it, already!"

Maria started to *not* drop it already, but then Mr.

Grigg appeared and tapped on the plate glass window.

Roly said, "I can put up with all the Bible thumping and the Bible food and the Bible stories as long as I know he's coming to get me. There's an end in sight."

Mr. Grigg flipped the sign around; MAIL: YES brushed the glass.

"There's always an end in sight," said Maria. "I know this because I'm a writer," she said. "The trick is to take that ending"—her hand grabbed a fistful of air—"and *twist* it!"

Inside the post office, Maria collected a hardware store sales flyer, an issue of *Scientific American* for her dad, plus a card for her grandma from an ancient sister in Oaxaca. Georgia had a letter, too, and they went back outside with their mail and sat on the curb to look it over.

Georgia opened the letter, and a new picture slipped from the folded page: Blythe in a yellow dress with a flared skirt and a raised wineglass in one hand; Rosemary in a purple-and-pink striped onesie, her rounded diaper bottom stretching the stripes. On the back of the picture Blythe had written, *Rosie, aged seven months. Chin-chin!*

Maria peeked at the picture. "Rosie's so cuuuute," she said, and then nodded at the paper in Georgia's hand.

"She say anything about the breathtaking work of art?"

Maria often "spiced up" the letters Georgia wrote to Blythe. The last one Maria spiced up had been, according to Maria, "terrifically exciting" and "wildly entertaining," with a "tearjerker of a PS."

PS: *I will never forget that pistachio sheet cake, how delicious it was and how green. And that time when you called me in sick from school so we could visit the aquarium when it wasn't crowded. And when you made me the genie Halloween costume with the gauzy pants and the golden tube top and the hairdo and didn't even make me cover it all up with a parka. And Freddy.* (Maria had given Georgia a strict limit of three memories, so she wasn't allowed to elaborate about Freddy. Or Blythe's beautiful singing voice. Or the way she smelled like roses.) *I miss you, I long for you.* (Maria couldn't decide which was better so she wrote them both for "double the impact," and declared the whole thing a "breathtaking work of art.")

Georgia leaned so she could tuck the picture in her back pocket, and then began to read the letter out loud. "'Dear Georgia, Rosie is adorable, isn't she? Last week I fed her peas and mashed potatoes. What a mess! She sleeps through the night, and is a joy and delight. Hey! I'm a poet and I didn't even know it!'" That part was cute. She looked up.

"This is the single most boring letter I ever heard," said Roly.

Georgia turned the letter over; there was more on the other side. "At least she wrote me back," Georgia said, skimming Blythe's neat cursive on the second page.

"When *my* mom writes me back, I have to duck and cover," said Maria.

"They sent me a recording of my ma reading a *bedtime* story one time," Georgia heard Roly say. "It was supposed to help me sleep, at the homes. A CD! How was I supposed to play a CD?" Roly sniffed noisily and Georgia glanced up from her letter. He spat in the dirt, as if to say *that* was what he thought of *that*.

"Disgusting," said Maria. "Do you want your defining feature to be 'boy who spits'?"

Georgia went back to reading her letter, which was longer than usual.

"Anyway, I'm too old for bedtime stories," she heard Roly say. She wasn't really listening.

"But not too mature," Maria said sweetly.

"So you know what I did with that stupid CD?"

"Stashed it in a velvet-lined box under lock and key? Sold it on the black market? Duplicated—"

"No, no, no—I threw it in the garbage."

Georgia gasped.

"So what?" Roly glared at her. "So I threw it away, big deal!"

"No, the letter, the letter!" Georgia gripped the letter in both hands as if it weighed ten pounds. "There's more," she said.

"What is it?" Maria said, alarmed. She grabbed Georgia's wrist. "Oh no. Did somebody die? Is it Lyle? Is it baby Rosie? It's Rosie, isn't it? She's sick. She's dying." Her hands flew to her cheeks. "Poor little Rosie; she's dead." Maria did not whip out her notebook, but Georgia could tell she wanted to.

"Who's dead?" Roly said.

"Nobody's *dead*." Georgia handed the letter to Maria and started to explain to Roly, "My mother—"

"*Shhhhhhh-shush!*" Maria hissed as she pushed up her eyeglasses. When she'd finished reading the letter— her speed-reading was as good as her shorthand—she closed her eyes and pressed the flowered notepaper to her chest.

"What's happening?" Roly said. "Did she talk about the breathtaking work of art?"

Maria's eyes popped open. "She did not; Blythe is a terrible correspondent," she said bitterly. "Really very bad. But this! This is . . . well, it's whacktastic!" Maria thrust the letter back to Georgia. "Don't you think? It's whacktastic?"

Georgia's heart was still pounding. "Yeah! Whacktastic!"

"*What's* whacktastic? C'mon, tell me!"

After being gone for half of fourth grade and all of fifth, Blythe was finally coming back for a visit. Here was the letter that said so. But where would Georgia start? What would she say? How long would Blythe stay? Would they pick right up where they'd left off? Where, exactly, had they left off? Georgia had so much to show her, to tell her, to *ask*. . . .

"This has nothing to do with you, Georgia," Blythe had said that day. "I love you, baby, but I *have* to leave, or else . . ." Blythe had looked at the house and then shot her arms up, as if tossing confetti at a party for unhappy people. "Or else I'll just *explode*!"

Georgia and her dad had watched the sporty blue sedan turn the corner and disappear, taillights winking as if the whole situation was just a funny joke, a prank, and then they'd gone inside the house. Later, he'd brought out a bunch of old games.

Glumly, they played Parcheesi and checkers. They played Go Fish and Old Maid. Then there was the game with the cartoon man's body and his red light bulb nose. *Operation! The Skill Game Where You're the Doctor*, it said on the box, along with a warning: *Make Cavity Sam Better, or Get the Buzzer!* Her dad hovered the metal tweezer above the cutouts in the body of Cavity Sam— the broken heart, the wrenched ankle—before deciding to remove the funny bone from Cavity Sam's elbow.

Bzzzzzzzzt! The nose lit up red and Georgia jumped.

"Sometimes," her father had said then, "people feel like they're going to explode on the inside." He'd briefly put his hand—rough, dry—over Georgia's. "Do you understand?"

She'd kept her eyes locked on Cavity Sam. Poor Cavity Sam, naked except for his underwear, with his insides all on view. Georgia was scared and embarrassed. "I might explode," she whispered, because it felt like a terrible secret. "I might explode into a million, zillion pieces."

Now Maria elbowed Georgia lightly in the rib cage. "Hey," she said. "What's with the tears?"

Georgia stared at the letter in her hands. "I'm just— I'm just—it's just so whacktastic!"

Roly yanked two handfuls of his own hair. "Is whacktastic *good* or *bad*? Can you at least tell me *that much*?"

Maria grabbed Georgia's arm and pulled. "My *abuelita* says there's nothing in the world that isn't better with cookies," she said. "Come on. Let's go to my house and jot down all your interesting feelings!"

"Can I come?" Roly's red hair was sticking out in clumps where he'd tugged it.

Maria cocked an eyebrow. It was Georgia's news to tell or not. Georgia hesitated—they'd known this boy all of a day and a half, and so far he'd stolen and lied. But she nodded; Roly grinned.

"Cookies!" he pumped a fist in the air. "Whacktastic!"

Chapter 5

They ran all the way to Maria's house and up a gravel path along the side of the house, to the back door. At the bottom of the steps, Maria's grandmother was sitting on the seat part of her walker, smoking a cigarette.

"Hola, *chiquitos*," she said. Smoke poured out of her nose and her mouth and hung around her head like a storm cloud gathering.

"Hola, MaLita," said Maria. She handed over the letter from Oaxaca, and plucked the cigarette out of her grandma's mouth with a practiced move.

"Hey!" Maria's grandma shouted, pouring out a puff of smoke. The dogs, sleeping in the sun, didn't even lift their heads. They'd seen it all before. Maria's grandma's face was a shade of gray-brown, like the house, and her skin was finely lined all over, like crepe paper. Georgia wanted to touch her cheek, it looked so soft.

"You're rotten, you know that?" the old woman said in Maria's direction.

"*Pfffff,*" Maria said to Roly, as if to explain the situation.

"Not you, Georgie," Maria's *abuela* added, smiling sweetly so that her eyes and cheeks crinkled. She brought the letter to her nose and sniffed. "You're not rotten. You neither," she said, looking at Roly. "Whoever you are."

"He's with us," said Maria.

"*Si, claro,* that much is clear."

"Ma Lita, meet Roland Park," Maria said. "Roland Park, meet my *abuela.*"

"Hello," said Roly. "Missus . . . *abuela,*" he added.

"You can call me Lita. I feel we can be casual. Grab me my smokes, Roland."

"Ignore that, Roly," said Maria.

"*Pfffff,*" said Lita. There was lots of *pffff*-ing going on. She banged a fist on the grip of her walker. "I don't have to be here, you know, Maria!"

They went up the ramp and in the door.

"Can you hear it? That cabana in Puerto Escondido's

calling my name!" Lita hollered. "I can go back home at any time! I can go tomorrow, maybe!"

At Maria's house, the kitchen walls were papered with scraps. Higher up on the walls the scraps were all in shades of brown; lower down, the papers were colored with crayons and Magic Markers and pencils and paint. It looked as if every bit of artwork and stickered quiz got taped to the walls. Some of it was Georgia's, since this was usually her home base during her dad's work hours. A map of the world used to be bright, with many hues. Now the map looked as if a stiff wind had come along and deposited a layer of dried leaves, curling at the borders of every nation.

Maria pushed aside a big plastic tub marked SARDINE SCHOOL to make room at the table. "My mama's got them working on banners and flags for the Fourth of July parade," Maria said, indicating the fabric and paints in the tub. Mrs. Garcia taught every summer at the school for the kids of Harmon Lobster's seasonal workers. There were Passamaquoddy kids from the other side of Maine, Mi'kmaq from Nova Scotia and New Brunswick, and kids from as far away as Florida and Mexico. Seasonal work had brought Mr. Garcia's family to Maine when he was a little boy.

Maria got out a package of cookies from a cupboard—

the wrapper read *polvorones*—and they sat down and passed them around. "So," said Maria. "Is she coming alone?"

"Who's she?" said Roly.

"Georgia's mother," said Maria. She put out her hand to demand the letter.

"What's happening?" said Roly.

Georgia slid the note across the table toward Maria.

"Coming from where?" said Roly.

"One year and eight months ago, my mother left town with Lyle Lenczycki," Georgia explained. "A man from her past."

Roly nodded as if he'd expected as much. As if such a thing was commonplace. Such a thing certainly was not commonplace for Georgia. It happened once only, but it felt like it continued happening every day.

Roly fished out another *polvorone* and ate it thoughtfully. Georgia wondered if his thoughts were about *his* mother, who had been declared unfit, and who would not be coming to visit him any time soon.

"She says here," Maria said, scanning the note, "it's a good time for a special visit. She says baby Rosemary should know her big sister. She says she misses you more than she can stand. She says you'll love Lyle, you'll absolutely love him. She says they'll see you on—" Maria whipped her head around to look at the Wink's Hardware calendar on the wall beside the fridge, and poked the air, counting. She whipped back around. "Holy moly, they'll be here in eight days!"

Roly studied the calendar. "Hey," he said, "do you want me to be there, Georgia? That's a Sunday, so—gosh, probably I'll have to miss church," said Roly. He tapped his chin. "Yeah . . . I really think I ought to be there for you." He rubbed his face all over as if he were really thinking hard about it. "You know, to help out my friend. I have to prove I have friends, or—"

Maria rolled her eyes. "We know, we know, or else they'll invite the whole Sunday school for a holy potluck and *make* you make friends."

Georgia crunched a cookie. She tried to picture the arrival of Blythe and baby Rosemary and Lyle Lenczycki. "I know the when," she said slowly, "I just don't know the how—how it's going to be." Whacktastic! she figured. But also a little scary.

"It's like a test at school," Roly said. "You just have to not think too much about it till it happens."

Maria shook her head as if she pitied Roly for being so nonsensical. "That is very poor advice." She pushed the sleeve of *polvorones*—only two left—across the table to Georgia.

A tall and gangly boy sauntered into the kitchen, bouncing a basketball. He caught it and jammed it under one arm. "Awww, Georgia, was that the very last cookie?" It was one of Maria's two older brothers. Martin was seventeen, with big hands and spaghetti arms and a brand-new driver's license, and with that a new phone for emergencies.

"Fowwy, Martin," Georgia said, her mouth full.

"*Welp*, I guess I'll just drive to the store, in that case." Martin gave a world-weary sigh, as if driving were nothing special and maybe even boring, and so was having his own phone. "Yup. Just have to get behind the wheel and go where the ol' road takes me."

"If I had my license, I'd be outta here so fast you'd eat my dust," Roly said in a tough voice.

"I'd drive from sea to shining sea," Maria said.

"I'd go meet my baby sister right this minute," Georgia said. She took the photo out and glanced at it again.

"Sure!" Martin said. "You all could carpool, make a day of it." He gave a sly smile. "*If* you had your licenses."

"Plus a car," Georgia added.

They all nodded. So many roadblocks.

"Who's this?" Martin said about Roly. He tossed him the basketball.

Roly caught the ball.

"Good reflexes," said Martin approvingly.

Maria said, "Roland Park, meet Martin Garcia, licensed driver, in case you couldn't tell." Martin whipped his license from a back pocket and briefly flashed it for everyone to appreciate. "Martin, this is Roland Park."

"Hey."

"Hey."

Maria looked from one to the other. No further words were spoken between the boys. "Well, that was a pleasant conversation!"

Martin shrugged.

Roly shrugged.

Suddenly, loud music blasted from another room, along with a lot of high voices. "Let's get out while we still can," Maria said over the music. "It's my sisters! All of them!" She pushed away from the table and hopped up.

Outside, Lita was sitting on her walker in the same spot. She'd got hold of another cigarette, and was energetically puffing away as if she'd gladly give it her last living breath.

"See ya later, Lita," said Maria as she tugged the cigarette from her grandmother's lips.

Lita banged a fist on her lap and shouted, "That cabana is calling my name, Maria!"

Georgia handed Lita the last cookie. She'd held it back just for her. "Bye, Lita."

"Bye, Georgie. Don't be a stranger," Lita said to Roly.

"Are there usually cookies?" said Roly.

Lita nodded. "Mmhmm. Count on it." She narrowed her eyes. "The question is," she said, slowly and deliberately, "can I count on *you*?" She pointed a bony finger at Roly, then mimed smoking a cigarette. Slowly, creepily, she winked.

"Uhhh . . . ," said Roly.

Maria yanked Roly away by the neck of his T-shirt. "Make good choices, Lita!"

Chapter 6

Blythe is coming back. Blythe is coming back. Mom. My mom. Blythe is coming back. All afternoon, Georgia hummed the whacktastic news inside her head. And she thought about the day Blythe left.

Georgia knew what to do that night, the first night without her. Her mom had said so, right out loud. Freddy represented Blythe's love—undying—for Georgia. So no matter what, that lizard better not die! Simple. She made a bargain with the universe: she would love Freddy and take better care of this lizard than anybody in the history of lizards, and then—eventually—Blythe would come back!

She had set up Freddy's tank with all the things he

needed to be happy—a piece of driftwood to climb on and hide under, a nice rock, a layer of sand to mimic the desert of his natural world, a lamp like the sun for him to bask in, and over the top a screen to keep him safe and sound. She gave him all the things a bearded dragon would need, and she read to him and sang to him, and even though he wasn't what anybody would typically call warm and cuddly, she found him to be funny and friendly and lovable. "It's not for nothing they call 'em the golden retrievers of lizards!" Patty van Winkle had said, possibly making it up.

And Freddy loved her back! He would turn at the sound of her voice. He enjoyed a game where Georgia would put out a line of blueberries and he would walk along and eat them. Sometimes they'd play it with raisins. Sometimes the two of them would sit side by side in the backyard and bask in the sun.

But then, last fall, Freddy lost his zest for life. He stopped enjoying the blueberries game. He didn't notice when Georgia came into the room. He didn't listen to a word she was saying. And since Freddy's well-being and Blythe's undying love were connected by an invisible thread, then Freddy's decline meant something bad for Freddy's health *and* Georgia's heart. Patty van Winkle assured her that bearded dragons go through natural slumps, that it didn't mean anything. But Georgia knew better. It meant maybe Blythe didn't love her. Maybe she wasn't ever coming back.

That's why Georgia wrote the note on the side of Freddy's tank. She *had* to give Freddy a better life. For his sake, and her own.

Now Georgia looked around her room at all her treasured things: the boxed set of the Chronicles of Narnia, the teeny-tiny glass pitcher and glass fit for a mouse or a fairy, a jewelry tree with three dangling necklaces, a kaleidoscope, and her collection of off-and-on journals.

She took out last year's journal from the bookcase and turned to a list she'd made. There were two columns: BuBbLe (Before Blythe Left) and BlAh (Blythe Away).

BuBbLE:
House full of sounds
Beautiful singing, daily
Piano morning, piano evening
Colors and candles on table,
    artfully mismatched plates
Fun, sloppy dance parties
Talking

BlAh:
Mostly ticking of the clock
    (addendum: BuBbLe Georgia
    never even knew that clock
    ticked out loud!)
Singing—none
No piano. Dusty piano. Piano =
    junk station
Stuff on table, non-dining
    related
Forced board games
Quiet
Tick. Tock. Tick

She put the journal back, heard the car pull up to the garage, heard the door slam. Heard her dad banging around the kitchen, getting supper on. Soon she'd go downstairs and tell him. *Blythe is coming back. Blythe is coming back.* But she didn't hurry. The news might make him sad.

Sometimes, when he didn't know she was watching, she caught him being sad. Head-in-his-hands sad. It scared her to see him that way. If he was sad, then there wasn't any room for *her* to be sad. When there are only two, she figured, you have to take turns. Like a seesaw. But when he was sad, she felt sad, too, and that's not how a seesaw works.

Georgia reached into the glass tank and stroked Freddy's triangle-shaped head, a thing he used to like her to do. "I bet you're ready for your yummy supper," she said, being very careful not to betray her disgust.

She picked up the kaleidoscope and brought it to her eye and turned the tube and watched the bits of colored plastic shift. Maybe cockroaches weren't so bad. Blythe was coming to see her, so she *must* love her, just like she said, even if Freddy *wasn't* living his best life. She sighed, and set the kaleidoscope down.

But—ew—he couldn't really like them, the cockroaches. Georgia had seen Freddy's throat pouch puff out when he felt threatened or afraid—a "tell," her dad called it, something that gives someone's inner thoughts away. She'd thought he might feel threatened by the cockroaches; *she* sure did. She was glad she didn't have a "tell" like Freddy's. Poor Freddy. Sometimes people should be allowed to keep their inner thoughts inner.

"Freddy?" Freddy didn't even turn his head. Was he looking a little pale? "I'm sorry about the . . ." She didn't want to say it. "The alternative nutritional food source."

She opened the cardboard box and sprinkled a serving of cockroaches into the tank, then replaced the screen.

"Supper!" came her father's call.

"Coming!" Georgia yelled over her shoulder. When she turned to the tank again, it looked like Freddy hadn't moved an inch. The cockroaches were gone.

"Freddy?" she said. He didn't move his thorny head. "I'm really sorry about the cockroaches."

Georgia's father set a baking dish on a hot pad in the center of the table, tossed his oven mitts aside, and sat down. It wasn't so much a hot pad as it was a stack of things that happened to be there, happened to be flat, and happened to protect the table from heat. Bills, magazines, recipes, countless clippings from the paper, most of them headlined *How-To*. His apron tonight was royal blue with text that said GOOD-LOOKIN' IS COOKIN'. Georgia's father was not too good-looking. He looked sort of pasty-white and dry, and so did supper. A crust of crunchy-looking Corn Flakes over the top of the casserole concealed whatever lurked beneath. It wasn't lobster. Even though he worked in the lobster business, they rarely ate lobster themselves.

Georgia's father elbowed a stack of books to one side of his place—*The Field Guide to Maine State Flora and Fauna*, *How to Macramé*, the *I Hate to Cook* cookbook, with a French-English dictionary on top—and spatula-d a portion onto Georgia's plate, where it landed with a plop.

"What is it?" There was just enough room for Georgia's plate among the binoculars and needle-nose pliers, the masking tape and colored pencils and different types of glue.

"Leftover parfait." He jerked his head at the French-English dictionary. "In French," he said, "*parfait* means *perfect*, as in 'a perfect end to the day.'"

Georgia watched hot steam rise. The steam was like the thoughts roiling in her head—kind of misty and changeable and hard to catch hold of. And if she let them, they'd just drift away and she wouldn't have to think about whose turn it was to be sad.

Maria had once written a "character study" of Stanley Weathers. According to Maria's character study, these collections and stacks and clippings—all this stuff on the table—were evidence that Georgia's dad was the best and most useful kind of character in fiction: *multi-dimensional*. Georgia had asked her if one single person could be the strong, silent type; a jack-of-all-trades; a student of life; *and* an absentminded professor, all in one. "Of course!" Maria had said. "Why not? Nobody is just one thing. That would be ridiculously boring. The more *character* in a character, the better!"

"Bon appétit," Stan said, supposedly in French. "Now we eat."

Her father's very short French poem—*Bon appétit, now we eat*—reminded her of Blythe's little poem in plain English. "A letter came today," Georgia blurted, with a glance at the family picture that still hung on the wall.

"Hmm?" He took a bite of casserole and slowly chewed.

"There's a new picture of her and Rosie." She'd start with the picture, then move on to the news that Blythe was coming to town. Georgia pushed the food around her plate so it would cool.

"Hmm."

Georgia set down her fork—she'd identified green beans, corn, salsa, and something fishy—and slid the photograph out of her back pocket. She put the picture on the table between them and swiveled it so he could see. Upside down, Blythe's yellow dress looked like a large and gorgeous daffodil. Upside down, Rosie looked even more like an Easter egg.

Georgia's dad didn't move to pick up the photo. He took another forkful of casserole while looking at it out of the corner of his eye as if he didn't want to commit to viewing it full on. He chewed and chewed some more. Finally he swallowed and shifted in his chair. "Pink of health," he said. "The baby." He circled his fork near the photograph. "Looks healthy."

Maria thought the quiet ways of Stanley Weathers signaled deep thought and a soulful heart. But Maria wasn't the one whose BlAh job it was to fill the silences.

"She's coming," Georgia said abruptly.

"How's that now?"

"Mom. Blythe." Georgia slid the letter across the table. "Says she's coming. Here. In eight days."

He stared at the letter. Then he stared up so intently

at something behind her that Georgia twisted in her chair to see—but there was nothing there. She turned back and he looked at her a long moment. She couldn't tell what he was thinking.

"Well," he said.

"Well what?"

"Well, well, well, it's a deep subject." It was a joke, but he wasn't really smiling.

Georgia's dad pushed away from the table and popped up and tugged loose his apron ties. Then he retied them. "I'll clean up." Now he was looking at a spot a couple inches above Georgia's head. "Go and do your homework."

"I don't have any *home*work." Plus, she looked at the food on her plate. Had she even taken a single bite? She looked at the clock above the sink. They'd been sitting together for all of about three minutes.

"Good, good. That's good," he said, and, just as suddenly and inexplicably as he'd popped up, now he plopped down. "School okay?"

"Dad!"

He startled.

"It's June fifteenth! Summer! Remember summer? No homework? No school?"

His eyes seemed to bring her into focus. "Right,

right," he said. "Sorry, I—long day with the lobsters."

Lobsters kept half the town busy at Harmon Lobster processing facility: "The pride of down east Maine." His work schedule was on the fridge, under a lobster-shaped magnet, written in vermilion red. *Vermilion* was Florence Deonn's "signature color," and Florence was the one who wrote it. Florence was the Harmon Lobster receptionist and she put red on everything. "If a person can't enjoy the little tasks of daily life, then, baby? Days are gonna be *long*."

"Dad, is it—is it okay? That she's coming?"

"Sure, sure, it's fine. It's fine!" He smiled, but the line between his eyebrows looked about as deep as the Grand Canyon. "Is it okay with *you*?"

Georgia nodded. She tried to read his eyes for what he might be really thinking. *What's going on in there*, Blythe used to say, tapping on the top of his head with a fingertip.

Georgia's dad hunched over the table and slowly finished eating the casserole on his plate, bite after bite after bite. The Grand Canyon stayed put between his eyes.

Georgia, Filler of Silences, did her job: "Maria's parents have drawn a perimeter," she said. Stories from Maria's house were always good to use. She told her dad all about Maria's parents and the perimeter, and the message in the bottle.

"Huh. That's funny," said Georgia's father, wiping his mouth with a paper napkin. "Your mother's more the *lightning*-in-a-bottle variety," he said.

What did *that* mean? Maria called Stan Weathers the mysterious type. But Maria liked mysteries, whereas Georgia didn't like them much at all.

Georgia's dad balled up the napkin and dropped it on the table beside his plate, then he leaned back in his chair and ran both hands over his head, back and forth. His hair stood up wildly all around the bald part on top, like a strip of fake fur from the Halloween section at So-Fine Fabrics. "Your mother . . . ," he began. Georgia held very still. "Sometimes she makes plans, you know, and she makes them so all of a sudden, they could hardly be called *plans* at all." He looked sharply at Georgia. "You understand."

With that, supper was over.

Parfait.

Chapter 7

What were they doing—Georgia and Maria—
following Roland Park into the pines? It
was eight o'clock in the morning, and Roly
had promised them adventure. In spite of being new to
the area around Prospect Harbor—or maybe, Georgia
thought, *because* of it—Roly had led them across the
railroad tracks and into unknown territory. Why had
they followed?

"Because look at his shirt!" said Maria.

For the third day in a row, Roland was wearing that
same T-shirt. KEEP ON TRUCKIN'.

"So?" Georgia said.

"So, we're keepin' on truckin'."

Maybe a message on a T-shirt was reason enough

for Maria to wander deep into the woods behind someone they'd basically only just met, but Georgia was
having second thoughts. Maria hardly ever had second
thoughts. And Georgia didn't want to stay behind, at
home with the letter and the news and her dad. He was
home all morning because he'd be on the late shift, and
she didn't want a repeat of last night: board games and
riddles. She'd slept with the letter and the picture under
her pillow; now she carried them in the back pocket of
her shorts.

So there they were in the woods, following Roland,
because he'd told them he found something good.

Maria stopped abruptly. Georgia knocked into her.
Maria pulled her notebook from her plastic flowered
bag. "I'm getting a lot of material here," said Maria.

Georgia took in the scenery in among the trees: a
couple tires, some smashed cans of probably beer, and
an empty jar with a grubby label: SOUWER PICKLES, A FAM-
ILY COMPANY. The air smelled of mold and muck. "For a
romance?"

"For a novel of suspense," said Maria. "This would
make an outstanding crime scene."

They walked for ten or twenty minutes, maybe more;
it was hard to tell. Georgia marched along to the beat of
the little tune in her head: *Blythe is coming back. Blythe*

is coming back. Mom. My mom. Blythe is coming back.
The ground was bouncy underfoot where years of pine
needles had fallen and collected. *Blythe is coming back.*
Blythe is coming back. Every so often, birdsong pierced
the air. Sweat dampened Georgia's hair around her forehead and ears and the back of the neck. Her arms and
legs felt sticky. *Blythe is coming back.* There was the
whine of a mosquito, and then it got her. Where were
they going? What was it Roly Park had found?

Well, they had cast their lot with Roly, never mind
they barely knew him. It was summer, and Georgia
wasn't about to be the one to say, "Turn back."

At last they came to a clearing. And in the clearing
was a little house.

They all three stared, silent.

The house was partly hidden by the scrubby trunks
and branches of sumac and chokecherry. All around
and over the house climbed green vines of wild clematis
laden with buds, many with points of paler green where
they promised to open soon, and the open ones emitted
a flowery, earthy scent Georgia couldn't tell if she liked a
lot or didn't like at all. The house had a foundation built
of rough granite that sparkled in places; what remained
of the roof and walls were built of glass. The entire struc-

ture was sullied with greenish grime, but sun found glass in spots so that the house glinted and winked through all the guck with something like sly gladness, as if to say, *You found me!*—Wink!—*You're here!*

Maria put a hand to her heart. "I have always longed to come upon an abandoned glass castle . . . ," she said breathily.

Roly said, "It's not a glass castle, *Maria*. I knew you'd say that; it's just a little house! This is not a fairy tale!"

It was not a castle. But it *was* made of glass, and they never knew it was there, and it definitely was abandoned.

They stepped carefully. It looked like a place where snakes and spiders would lurk. In fact, there were a lot of impressive webs, and one spider that Georgia, uneasy, admired for its large size and red stripes.

"Nobody's been here in a long time," said Roly. He batted away the web, and the red-legged spider plopped to the ground and scuttled away.

"Now I don't know where it is," said Georgia about the spider.

"But we know where it isn't," said Roly.

Maria dropped her flowered plastic bag and began pulling away at the vines. "It's as if Mother Nature loved this glass castle," said Maria, "and covered all the broken parts with green, green, green."

"Oh, brother," Roly said.

Georgia stretched tall and clawed at what she could see—one upper corner, a hinge.

"And nary a soul has entered this place," Maria said softly, "not for a hundred years."

"Gah!" Georgia jumped: A big section of vines all came away as one, and Roland was standing in a doorway where the vines had been. Georgia rocked back. "How'd you get in?"

Roly jerked his thumb at the metal frame of a panel that had been broken out, the glass inside on the flagstone-and-dirt floor of the house. Remnants of broken glass still clung to the metal track of the structure.

"Where God closes a door," said Roly, "he opens a window. Or so I have heard fourteen times in the past three days." He bent and picked up some candy wrapper litter and stuffed it in his pocket. Georgia was surprised to hear him hum a little bit of a tune.

Maria got up from the ground and swept her arms in all directions. "Georgia," she said, "let us now step through the magical door!" She shot a look at Roly. "Properly!"

Inside the glass house it was warm, and the light was

tinged with green. Thick vines and thin saplings grew up and over the pointy ridge at the top of the house. Green things even grew straight up from the floor. Georgia expected to feel like she was breaking the law or something, but it didn't feel like trespassing, not at all.

Maria dropped her flowered tote and hugged herself. "It *is* like we walked into our very own fairy tale! I'm sorry, but I have to disagree with you, Roly."

"You're not sorry," Roly said.

"That's true, I'm not," said Maria.

Georgia reached both hands up, up, up. She would have to grow quite a bit to reach the roof. For some reason—because of all the glass, and being inside it— Georgia thought of Maria's message in the bottle, and so, also, she thought about the thing her father had said about her mother. It seemed, with the glass all around and the three of them inside, as though they'd stepped over a threshold and *into* a bottle. Georgia could easily imagine the three of them had shrunk. She dropped her arms to her sides. "What's—lightning in a bottle?"

Maria said, "It means *elusive*," as if Georgia's question were perfectly unsurprising and had come about for good reason. "Something that can't be contained."

"Like Maria's personality," said Roly.

"Why, *thank* you," said Maria.

Roly blushed. "I didn't mean it as a *comp*liment, Maria!" he said. "And it's not a *fairy tale*, it's a cool secret hideout, okay?" Roly kicked at a shard of broken glass and sent it skidding.

Maria put her hand to her heart. She was doing a lot of that. "We two are princess cousins, and this," she pointed daintily at Roly, "is the prince from far away, who will vie for our attention."

"Gross," Roly said.

"Yuck," Georgia said.

"All right already, fine; Roland, you can just be another cousin." Maria looked miffed. "We can *alllll* be cousins. Fine." Her face lit up again. "Three good-looking-but-distant cousins who escape their obnoxious families and make a new life, forsaking all their royal . . ." She looked up at the glass roof for a second. "Their royal *spiffiness*," she went on, "and saying *adieu, adios,* and *sayonara* to everything that made them who they are."

Roly stared at Maria, shaking his head.

She lifted her shoulders, palms up—*what's the problem?*

That afternoon, they cleared out dead leaves. They pulled weeds and picked up sticks. Georgia cut her finger on a shard of glass but it wasn't too bad, and Maria carried Band-Aids in her tote bag. They all got very dirty.

Roly would have to wear a different shirt after this, Georgia figured. But that was the first thought she'd *noticed* in a while . . . how long, she couldn't tell, because it was the kind of day when time didn't make itself known. Even the movement of the sun seemed pointless in terms of a clock or a watch or a box on a calendar page. There was meaning all around, a richness attached to nothing in particular, nothing they could name. Was it the glass that made this place and this time seem important? Was it that they'd never known about this place or who built it or why, and so they felt free to claim it? Old and new and hidden and visible—and fragile—all at once.

Georgia felt full and brimming over with insight and calm. She tried to put the feeling into words. "It's like—having everything right."

Maria blinked. "You're a natural poet," she said.

Roly—even Roly!—nodded in agreement. "I like how it's hidden away so nobody can take it. Nobody can come in here and crap all over it."

"Gee. Pure poetry," Maria said.

"I can't wait to show my brother," Roly said, ignoring Maria's jab.

"What's his name, this brother?"

"Name?" Roly looked flustered, caught. "Uh, Preston."

"Preston Park?"

The mention of someone coming gave Georgia the shivers all over again. *Blythe is coming!* She slid the letter from her pocket and stared at the words. It hardly mattered what the letter said or didn't say.

"Yeah. Preston Park."

Georgia ran her fingertips over the paper. Blythe had written those words, with her hand, the same hand she had used, before, to cup Georgia's cheek or rub her back.

"Continue," said Maria.

Georgia glanced up from the letter in her hands.

Roly was looking at Maria like she was loony.

"She's just naturally curious about others," Georgia said, slipping the letter into her pocket.

"Yeah, well, you'll get to see him in person if you're lucky."

Maria clicked her pen. "What do you mean, lucky? Is he very handsome?"

"No! I don't know! I just mean—when he turns eighteen and comes to get me, maybe you'll *see* him."

Now Georgia tugged the photo from her pocket.

"And when is that again?"

"What?"

"When he's coming to get you?"

Roly looked befuddled. He really didn't seem to have

a lot of experience answering questions. Or maybe he'd been asked too many, or too many times.

"August—I told you, August first!"

"You should get him a present."

"How come?"

"For his birthday, August first." Maria dropped her notebook in her tote.

"Oh. Right." He rubbed his chin, thinking. "Are there any good stores in this Podunk, backwater . . ."

Georgia heard Roly and Maria saying words . . . Podunk . . . presents . . . but she wasn't listening; she was looking at the picture of Blythe in her daffodil-yellow dress, and baby Rosie in her Easter-egg stripes. Georgia couldn't remember being a baby, but she could remember being her mother's daughter. If she had a defining feature, maybe that was it.

When they came out of the pines and before they parted, they agreed again that they wouldn't tell a soul about the glass house.

"Swear on it," Roly said. He spit on his palm and held out his hand to shake.

"Disgusting," said Maria, and crossed her arms.

"You can take our word for it," Georgia said.

Roly shrugged—*I guess*—and wiped his hand on his

ribs. "Well, smell ya later," he said. He hooked a thumb under each armpit and waggled his fingers.

"Revolting," said Maria.

They watched him walk away toward who knows where.

"What do you guess he's going to do all day?" Georgia said to Maria.

Maria squinted after him. "Probably not study the Bible."

They watched Roly go a ways down Belmont, and turn the corner onto Harbor Drive.

"You think he really has a brother, Preston Park, aged near eighteen, coming to get him?"

"Sure!" Georgia thought about it. "You don't believe him?"

"He was very shifty about it, that's all I'm saying." Maria poked up her glasses. "Poor kid. Even if ours have moved out—to Massachusetts, or the Scamp . . ." Maria glanced at Georgia. "At least nobody's declared *our* mothers unfit."

Blythe is coming back. Blythe is coming back. Mom. My mom. Blythe is coming back. The giddy little tune played again in Georgia's ears. A thought crossed her mind as she walked the last bit home along Garden Street: the glass house wasn't a place where her mother had been and *wasn't* anymore. Was it a thrilling thought? A lonesome thought?

It was just a thought.

Chapter 8

The day Blythe returned, Georgia waited at the window and watched for the car that would bring her, the car that belonged to Lyle Lenczycki. Puffy clouds hung like solid things, unmoving as bricks. The sky was as blue as the sky can be, fixed in place as if it were a painting and not real. It seemed to Georgia that the clouds should be speeding across the sky, racing like her heart, and changing shapes before her eyes.

She had put on yellow shorts and a white T-shirt with yellow stripes. Blythe loved yellow. Georgia's stomach was in knots and so was her hair. She'd asked Maria to come over to fix it, but she was on baby duty. Her father had brushed it and made it worse; now it was knotted and also frizzy and puffy. Georgia had hoped to look nice today of all days.

Her father hadn't tried at all. He had on an apron spattered with stains. The apron was printed with a message: HEISLER—IT'S A GOOD-DRINKIN' BEER. That apron did not seem at all appropriate.

Georgia kept watch in the front room. She was sitting on her knees on the couch, peering over the back of it between the Venetian blinds and out the window.

After a long while, a blue car came up the road and stopped in front of the house. The passenger door opened.

Out came Blythe.

There she was.

Georgia waved.

Blythe slammed the passenger door with one hip.

Georgia gathered herself and scrambled off the couch. Her heart beat fast. She stood up straight and smoothed her hair and her shirt and shorts and even the skin of her knees. Suddenly she wished she knew something—anything—about toenail polish, a thing she'd never thought of all her life. She looked down at Freddy. He looked particularly green today, almost electric. She picked him up. "Here we go, Freddy."

Georgia's father met her at the front door. He still had

on that dumb apron, and now he'd flung a damp-looking dish towel over one shoulder.

Georgia chewed her cheek.

Her father reached out a hand toward Georgia, but didn't quite touch. He let his hand drop. "It'll be okay," he said.

"I know that!" Georgia snapped; she couldn't tell why. She set Freddy on the floor and put her hands on her hips. "It'll be whacktastic!" She practically shouted the word.

Georgia's father pressed his lips together. He took one step closer to Georgia, and put a hand on her shoulder. He patted it a couple times. Then he peered out the peephole and opened the door before Blythe could ring the bell.

Blythe stepped right in. Georgia held her breath.

Blythe screamed—not Georgia's name, not with joy.

It seemed the clock stopped. There was Freddy, frozen with his beard puffed out. There was Blythe's scream hanging in the air like a comic strip bubble. There was Georgia's dad in his stupid apron advertising beer. There was Georgia standing somehow outside of herself and watching it all, not knowing what to do. Maria would know, or invent something, but Georgia could only hold her breath and wait.

"Freddy! Freddy, you scared me!"

Georgia breathed out. Breathed in. Time went on.

"He's big now," Georgia said, because he was a foot long, and last time Blythe had seen Freddy he was just a baby. She instantly wished the first thing she'd said to her mother was something better. "He's reached full maturity," she said. That thing wasn't any better.

"My, my," Blythe said, still eyeballing Freddy.

"He won't bite," her father added.

"Says who?" said Blythe. She gave a tinkling laugh and fanned her face. Then, "Oh, my *darling* darling!" she cried, and took Georgia by the shoulders. "Look at you! I've missed you so much. I love you so much." Then she pulled Georgia to her and held her so tightly Georgia could barely breathe but hardly cared—she might die right then and there in her mother's arms. Maria could write about it: *And Georgia died happily ever after*.

Blythe smelled like roses. "Oh, I've missed you, Georgie!" She released Georgia and held her at arm's length again and gazed into her eyes. Tears! There were tears in Blythe's eyes, tears for Georgia. Georgia felt her own tears coming; it would be okay if she cried now that Blythe was.

Blythe sniffed and turned away, ducking her chin to one shoulder. "Stan," she said. She hesitated, then opened her arms to him and then he opened his arms, and after a couple false starts, they hugged. The dish towel plopped to the floor, and Stan bent in half to pick it up. He made a humming sort of noise from where his head was, down around his knees. It was taking him longer than would be expected to collect the towel from the floor.

"It's good to see you, Stan," said Blythe to the top of Stan's head.

When he stood upright, Georgia's parents stared at each other a long moment, which was broken by the sound of the doorbell.

"Oh!" said Blythe. "I forgot Lyle!" She opened the door wide and standing there was a man so handsome he might have stepped straight out of the TV, or hopped down from an alabaster pedestal. His dark hair was perfectly parted and swept back from his brow in a thick, glossy wave. His white skin was bronzed by the sun, and his teeth were blinding. He wore a black button-up shirt tucked into sharp blue jeans. He looked like he was the one they had in mind at the factory when they made that other apron: *Good-Lookin' Is Cookin'*. He carried over one shoulder a large quilted bag printed all over with ducks. His other arm cradled a baby.

Georgia took her all in at once. The pastel stripes

and polka dots; the sunlight catching on her hair, fine and—baby fine! That's where that term came from! Her baby-fine hair fluffed like cotton candy spun from gold; pudgy legs kicking—what a funny word, *pudgy*; eyes huge and round and bright, clear blue; skin pink-white. Her big head jounced around—yanked from thing to thing to thing, her attention on a string—and then her gaze met Georgia's. Her eyes said at once *Who are you?* and *I know you.*

The others were speaking, but their talk seemed elsewhere and nonsensical, like chatter in a tree. Georgia felt loose from her body; she might float to the ceiling.

The baby huffed and puffed and kicked her pudgy legs. Then she was twisting and lunging with both arms, and Georgia opened her arms without thinking.

Strange: a moment—a split second—a memory of being a baby herself came quick, and then she had this baby, her baby, in her arms.

"Meet your baby sister, honey!"

Georgia's senses flooded. She could hardly sort her feelings; her thoughts came all pell-mell. Rosie was squishy and solid and heavy, much heavier than she looked. Georgia was afraid she'd drop her. The effort of holding required her whole body. Georgia scooched Rosie up higher on her hip, bouncing her knees, planting her feet. Every muscle grabbed hard around every bone, while her heart flipped and flooped as if something was medically wrong. Would she faint? Was she *dying*? Probably not.

She'd never even held a baby before, not even Matilda. There were always so many open arms at the Garcias', so the chance hadn't come up, or the notion that she could do it. Matilda wasn't her baby sister, after all. Rosemary was hers. Rosemary was her baby.

Rosie squirreled around and pushed against Georgia's chest and looked straight into Georgia's face. Very close. Cross-eyed close. She was huffing and chuffing, close to laughter. A quick hand swatted Georgia's mouth; little fishhook fingers caught her lip. Georgia nibbled the fingers; Rosie laughed as if from deep inside the earth. She let go of the pinched lip, curled into Georgia's body, sucked on her fist, and pointed at stone-still Freddy.

Georgia pressed her cheek to Rosie's head; it warmed her skin astonishingly. Slowly she rubbed her cheek on the soft, soft hair, closed her eyes and breathed, breathed. She smelled so good. Georgia tried to recognize the good smell of her. What was it? Sugar and spice and everything nice, went that dumb rhyme; sugar and spice and the meaning of life. The meaning of life, the point.

Georgia's eyes popped open. Rosie was heavy because of all that *life*. Blythe had told her nobody could know the meaning of life until they were very old. But she was wrong. Georgia knew it now, and suddenly.

"I'm sorry," Lyle Lenczycki was saying. He and her father were shaking hands. Greetings were going on, and no one seemed at all aware that Georgia had been somewhere else. She hiked up Rosie on her hip.

Stan said, "Hello."

"Yes, I meant hello," said Lyle, "that's exactly what I meant." He was still pumping Stan's hand up and down. The ducky bag slid down his arm and caught at his elbow.

Lyle quit shaking Stan's hand, dropped the diaper bag to the floor, and reached out for Georgia's hand, but both of hers were full of baby Rosemary. Lyle hovered his arms in space for a second, then crossed them over his chest. He put his hands on his hips instead. For such a good-looking person, he seemed pretty ill at ease. "It is a very great pleasure to meet you at last," he said.

"Georgia, meet your stepfather, Lyle."

Stepfather. Georgia hadn't thought of that. Step. Father. She maneuvered Rosie to her other hip.

"Hi," said Georgia.

When Lyle smiled, he had dimples on both cheeks.

"Now you have *two* fathers," said Blythe.

"The more the merrier!" said Lyle Lenczycki.

Says who? Georgia thought, echoing Blythe about Freddy and whether or not he'd bite.

Lyle blushed. There was a silence in which Georgia could imagine Maria jotting a note: *Pink became him.*

Stan tossed his dish towel back onto his shoulder in a careless-looking way. *Nonchalant! Bon appétit!* "None taken," he said, as if someone had suggested he take no offense.

Lyle Lenczycki put out his hands toward Georgia. "Shall I take Rosie? She's heavy after a while, am I right or am I right?"

Georgia was reluctant to give her up to Lyle, but he was right; her arms were tired. Rosie threw her head back and smiled gummily up at Lyle and gurgled and grabbed his chin. "Cheeky monkey," said Lyle fondly. "Not a care in the world." He smiled again at Georgia with both dimples on full blast. "Let me know when you'd like to hold her again. Rosie loves you already, I can tell." The dimples deepened.

"Of course she does!" Blythe sang. "What's not to love?" She cupped Georgia's cheek.

Georgia's father cleared his throat. "Where are you folks staying? How long are you in town?"

"Oh!" Blythe's hands flew to her lips; Georgia's whole body tilted, as if Blythe had been holding her up by her chin. "Didn't I tell you?" Blythe looked first at Stan and then at Georgia. "We've gone all in! We signed a lease on a house over on Belmont Street!"

The dish towel fell off Stan's shoulder. This time he didn't pick it up. He took a step closer to Georgia.

Blythe tugged a key chain from her purse, a tiny blue-and-green globe—planet Earth—and dangled it. Everyone looked at the key chain as if it were a rabbit she'd pulled from her purse. Rosie gurgled.

Georgia felt like there were marbles rolling around in her stomach. She looked again at the key chain. Like *worlds* rolling around. She was either going to giggle or blubber like a baby—out of control either way.

Blythe's eyes glittered with tears. "Oh, Georgie. Oh, my mascara!" she said, dabbing her eyes, laughing. "I'm just so glad. So very, very glad to be a family again."

Lyle Lenczycki bounced Rosemary gently up and down, and she chortled and patted his cheeks. "That's right, isn't it, Rosie? We're staying for good!"

Chapter 9

"Girl time!" Blythe sang, waving one arm and cradling Rosemary in the other as Lyle's car backed out of the driveway, then headed down Belmont Street with a *toot-toot* of the horn.

Goooodbye, Georgia said in her head. The moving van had come and gone the day before, and she was now glad to see Lyle's taillights disappear too.

Blythe gave Rosie a squeeze and a kiss, then leaned away enough so she could focus on her face. "Lyle's territory covers the entire Eastern Seaboard," she said, "which is very impressive. Lyle is a highly competent salesman." She licked her fingers and tidied Rosie's baby-fine hair. "But if I'm honest," she said, "he leaves me lonely half the time!" Rosie made a concerned face, as if she was looking inward and trying to solve all the world's problems.

Blythe glanced at Georgia. "She's pooping. That's her pooping face; cracks me up!"

"I can change her," Georgia said.

"Sweeter words were never spoken!" Blythe said, and laughed. "Have I told you lately that I love you?"

Georgia followed Blythe inside, past some boxes yet to be unpacked. Maybe Lyle would have an accident— not such a bad one, just enough to give him amnesia and then he'd forget to come back. That's exactly what happened to a person on Lita's soap opera, which was in Spanish and called something like *Rich People Cry, Too*. Or if amnesia was too TV-like, then maybe . . . his *appendix* could rupture—somewhere in Maryland, or Connecticut. Maybe he'd be stuck in a hospital long enough that Blythe would see they were better off without him. Those were two excellent, jot-worthy ideas right off the top of her head! Given more time, Georgia could imagine plenty of scenarios to get Lyle out of the picture. Out of town. Out of their lives. And then, with no Lyle, there would be no reason why Blythe and her dad couldn't get back together. No reason at all! She knew it was wishful thinking . . . but wasn't it wishful thinking that brought Blythe back to Prospect Harbor?

Blythe set Rosie gently on the changing table in the room they'd set up as the nursery. "There we go, Rosie-toes," she said in a sweet and singsong voice. She made funny faces at Rosie and tickled her tummy while talking softly to Georgia. "I'll do the cleaning up part this time and you can put on the fresh diaper. I don't want you to be traumatized by the horror that is a loaded diaper!" She made an *eek* face over her shoulder at Georgia.

Georgia clutched a diaper and stood by, watching Blythe unsnap Rosie's romper, peel back the diaper tapes, lift Rosie's pudgy legs with one hand, and use wipes to clean her bum with the other, all the while cooing and murmuring and clucking to Rosie's obvious joy and delight. In short order, the dirty diaper was all rolled up tight and thrown away.

"That wasn't too bad," Georgia said.

"Oh, I'm an expert diaper-changer," Blythe said, bicycling Rosie's little legs. "Isn't that right, Rosie-toes?" Rosie made happy huffing noises. "Watch this; she loves this." Blythe lowered her head slowly, slowly toward Rosie. Rosie's eyes grew huge, and she kicked her legs; Blythe blew a raspberry on her soft, round tummy, and Rosie laughed and laughed. It was so funny! Blythe stood aside, wiping tears of laughter from her eyes. "She just can't get enough of that—it's too funny. You try."

Georgia took Rosie's little feet in her hands—so soft, so small—and churned her legs in gentle circles. Then she leaned in—Rosie kicked her legs and huffed and chuffed; she knew what was coming—and gave her a big, loud raspberry. Rosie laughed and laughed. Her tummy was unbelievably soft and squishy.

"See? She loves it. You know who else used to love having her diaper changed?"

"Me?"

"Yup! Just like your sister." Blythe showed Georgia how to put on the fresh diaper and then Georgia snapped up the romper and patted that tummy again, picked Rosie up from the changing table, and rubbed noses with her. "She smells so good."

"I know! Isn't that the best, most wonderful smell in the world?" Blythe said. "But try to describe it—you can't! The only name for how a baby smells is: baby." She smiled at Georgia, then kissed the top of her head. "I swear I can still smell it on you, Georgie." She began to hum a little tune Georgia thought she recognized. "Moon river, wider than a mile . . . ," Blythe sang.

Georgia's heart fluttered.

"Two drifters, off to see the world . . . ," Blythe's

voice was clear and sweet and high. "There's such a lot of world to see. . . ."

Now Georgia was almost sure she remembered. "Did you sing that to me? When I was a baby?"

"Of course I did!" Blythe kissed Rosie's cheek, then Georgia's. "My babies."

A huge wave of love washed over Georgia and into her and out of her. It was so sudden, so over-whelming, she had to lean against the changing table to catch her balance. She was her mother's daughter, her sister's sister, and they were a family. It was almost—almost—perfect. She just wanted her dad in the picture, too. She wanted them all to be together. And when they were, Georgia would know that good feeling she'd had at the glass house again, the feeling of having everything right.

The next days, staying with Blythe, sped by in a whirl-wind. There was the trip to the mall to buy clothes. There was the double-feature movie at the Magic Lantern—Florence Deonn babysat Rosie—including all the buttered popcorn Georgia could eat, plus a root beer. There was the dance party in the kitchen of the house on Belmont, the music blasting.

And when a slow song came on, Georgia held Rosie

in her arms, swayed side to side and around and around, and bounced her gently up and down, as if she were a painted carousel pony and Rosie her passenger. Rosie put her little hand on Georgia's cheek and gazed into her eyes, and Georgia thought she could see her baby sister's very soul in there. Rosemary seemed wise and older than her months. Georgia's stomach lurched. She was giddy and happy and a tiny bit sick. This is love, Georgia thought. I love my baby sister. I love her like a mountain or a sunset or a lake—something large, something that just *is*.

On Thursday, Blythe stopped Georgia at the front door. "Where are you going?"

"I just need to check on Freddy again," Georgia said. She'd been checking on him every day. "And it's been nearly a whole week since I've seen Dad or my friends."

"A whole week?" said Blythe. "A wee little, teeny little week? You don't see me for going on two *years*! I'm your mother, newly returned! The Prodigal Mom!" Blythe regarded Georgia, one hand propping her chin. "Georgie, I know you want to see your father and your special friends—the foster boy and Maria-whose-parents-live-in-a-trailer—but"—her hands flew—"don't you want to know what *my* plans were for today?" Blythe made a funny pouty face, and drew Georgia back into the living room. "Think of Rosie! Rosie wants to be with you."

Georgia knelt beside Rosie's bouncy chair on the floor. She wiggled Rosie's tiny little pinky toes, and Rosie babbled and breathed fast and bounced. Then Georgia looked up at her mom. "So! What are we doing today?"

Blythe borrowed a car from an old high school friend for the short drive to the ocean. "I cannot believe Heidi's old hatchback is still chugging along—but after all, high school wasn't *that* long ago." First they swung by the house on Garden Street so that they could bring Freddy along for some fresh air.

Stan was sitting at the dining room table, a deck of cards arranged before him in a row of cascading stacks. The house smelled of sleep. "Stan, it's nine thirty in the morning! What are you doing playing solitaire in your pajamas?"

"Day off," he said. Two words. Was he the strong, silent type, or just rude? Couldn't he make a little conversation here?

Blythe ruffled his hair; he drew back from her hand. "You look like you stuck your finger in a light socket, Stan." Blythe winked at Georgia, as if the two of them knew something he didn't. Georgia wasn't sure what the something was. She wished he had on that nice shirt he got for Florence Deonn's wedding last summer. That looked good on him.

Georgia held Freddy gently, cupping his belly with her palm and fiddling with the little harness she'd made for him when he'd got full grown, so she could walk him on a leash. He looked ready for adventure. "Thanks for feeding him yesterday," she said.

Stan nodded. "No trouble." Stan's tired eyes moved to Georgia. "See you tonight?" he said. "Cowboy lasagna."

Georgia looked at her feet; for some reason, she felt a flash of anger.

"Georgia?" he said. "Everything okay?"

"Yeah!" Georgia said, facing him. "Everything's great!" Stan lifted his eyebrows as if asking a question. Georgia glanced again at Blythe, and back to her father. "What?" she snapped. He looked down at his cards. She realized why she was mad. How was she going to get them back together if he wouldn't even try?

They tumbled out of the hatchback at Prospect Harbor Light—Freddy and Rosie and Georgia; insulated cooler bag; picnic blanket; and from the driver's side, Blythe.

"Have you ever seen a bluer sky?" she cried.

Georgia thought of all the shades of blue in her dad's can of pencils on the table—azure, cornflower, ocean-view; deep sea, mystic sapphire, Dresden plate. Clouds were everywhere—thunderheads that awed but didn't threaten; endless and puffy white. Sunlight sparkled on the waters of the Atlantic as far as the eye could see, and Prospect Harbor Light looked important and ready to warn or to welcome. Island roses fluttered delicate pink among the rocks; the delicious summer smell of them came on strong with every blast of wind.

They picked their way along the paths above the rocky coastline. Blythe even walked Freddy on his leash so that Georgia could carry Rosemary. She held the leash daintily, with her pinky up.

"Have you got your period yet?"

"Yuck! Mom! No!" Georgia felt her face get hot, and not from the sun. She was grateful for the cooling salty air.

"Well, thank goodness I'm here for you when it happens," Blythe went on. "I can only imagine how Stan would handle one of the most important transitions in a young woman's life."

Georgia *had* imagined it. She dreaded the day she'd get her period and have to tell her father. She'd planned out several different scenarios, and each plan failed badly in her mind's eye. One scenario she'd envisioned was over a game of Operation. "Dad, I've got my period." *BBbbbzzzzzzt!*

"It'll be fun," said Blythe. "We'll *celebrate*! I'll take you for a fancy-pants lunch at Pomodoro's in Portland. I love that place, don't you? The spaghetti carbonara? And I'll buy you a new dress . . . we can even get our toenails done. Would you like that?"

"I guess." Rosemary's head nodded and dropped, heavy on Georgia's chest.

Blythe looked at Freddy, at the other end of the leash. "He's actually kind of cute, isn't he? Hi, Freddy! Hi, Fred!" she said. "Speaking of cuties, I bet that boy Roland Park has some secrets. I bet he likes you!"

"Mom!"

"What? Of course he likes you. What's not to like?"

Georgia had only just stopped blushing about her period, and here she was blushing all over again! It would be scary if Roly *liked* her liked her. What would she do? She put her cheek to Rosie's head, but the warmth only made her skin burn hotter. If Roly liked anybody, it was probably Maria. Maria had so many things to say and was never afraid.

They had come to a grassy spot protected from the

wind; Blythe spread the picnic blanket, plopped down, and patted the space beside her. "Oh, what a day," she sang. "Tell me everything, baby. Tell me allllll your secrets!"

"I don't have any secrets," Georgia said. She lowered drowsy Rosie onto the blanket, and sat down beside her.

"Oh, come on now, everybody has secrets." Blythe got out a bottle from the cooler bag and gave it to Rosemary. "At least one good, juicy secret. Every person on earth. Even babies, probably," she said. "I hate mashed peas," she sang in a baby voice. "I wuv bananas!" She folded up the brim of Rosie's sun hat and made a googly face at her. "But that's not much of a secret, is it, Rosie-toes?"

Georgia watched Rosie drink her bottle. In a few moments her milky lips loosened, the bottle slipped to one side, and she was asleep. Georgia carefully removed the bottle from Rosie's little hands and tucked it away in the cooler bag.

"Okay," Georgia said; she didn't want Blythe to be displeased. "Here's a secret. Roland Park stole a cat collar." Immediately Georgia felt terrible.

"Well, well, well," said Blythe. "A little thief. How spunky."

"You have to promise not to tell!" Georgia said.

"Honey, trust me, I won't tell. Besides, who would care?"

Roly, for one, Georgia thought.

"Oh, would you look at that face!" Blythe cried, cupping Georgia's chin. "You poor little worrywart. Poof! I've already forgotten." She winked. Then she stretched back onto the blanket beside the sleeping Rosemary. "What a glorious day to be us." Blythe waved her arms toward the sky, slowly weaving her hands in a dance.

Georgia lay back on the blanket beside her. Freddy snoozed in the sun.

"Listen, sweetie," Blythe said. "When I left . . ." She turned her head to look into Georgia's eyes. "You *must* know how it broke my heart to leave you." She pressed her lips together, holding back emotion. "I could never stand to say goodbye again."

Georgia had never thought about it that way . . . that *Blythe's* heart might have broken when she left, just like Georgia's. She felt for her mother's hand. Blythe took it and squeezed. "I'm going to make it up to you, baby," she whispered fiercely. "Cross my broken heart."

Chapter 10

P *fffft* went Roly. "That's what they all say."
Georgia and Maria and Roly—and Freddy—were
on the green in front of the library. The day was
already warm and on its way to hot. Clouds to the east
mumbled about rain.

"Blythe's different!" Maria said. "Shopping at the
outlet mall, the sleepovers, yesterday at the bay, the
lobster rolls—and look at that hair!" Maria touched
Georgia's hair with her fingertips as if it might break
or be sticky. Blythe had styled it yesterday with a round
brush, a blow-dryer, and some kind of spray that held it
in place even though she'd slept on it. "Blythe Is Back!
B-I-B!" Maria yelled, which caused Freddy's beard to
puff out beneath his little harness.

"Sorry, Freddy," Maria said.

Suddenly Roly ducked. "You guys!" he said in a loud whisper. "Do *not* at*tract* at*ten*tion." That would be tricky: a boy wearing—again!—a fairly filthy KEEP ON TRUCKIN' T-shirt and crouching on the grass, beside him a large lizard in a colorful vest.

Across the green, beyond the tent stalls of the farmers' market, Mrs. Farley and Winslow could be seen going up the steps of the town hall. Mrs. Farley disappeared inside as Winslow, trailing behind her and tugging on his shorts, waved an arm high overhead.

"Ignore him," said Roly.

Georgia waved anyway. "Why are you hiding from your fosters?" Maria said as she waved too.

"I'm not hiding," Roly said. His voice was muffled because of his chin being tucked to his chest and his arms covering his head.

"You are, too, hiding," Maria said. "You look like a turtle."

Winslow's attention was drawn from within the town hall—maybe Mrs. Farley had called to him—and he gave another wild wave and hopped inside.

"He's gone; you can come out of your shell now," said Maria. Roly stood up and dusted off his shorts.

"You want to know what he *did*?" Roly made a fist.

"*Baby* brothers—even *temporary* ones—are the worst!"

"You're a baby brother," Georgia observed, scooping Freddy up and settling him to ride on her shoulder.

"Aha!" Maria grinned and pointed her finger in the air. "Per*spec*tive!"

"That's different! I'm not a *baby*," he spat, "and I'm a *great* brother. Just wait till Preston shows up; Preston'll tell you."

Maria hitched her flowered tote up her arm and cast a sly, sidelong look at Georgia. She nodded almost imperceptibly, lifted her eyebrows, and mouthed the letters *M-O-P*. Maria had come up with a theory she called the Myth of Preston.

Elements of the MoP so far included:

No photographic evidence.
Does not like to talk about him; refuses when pressed.
Struggled to say name, Preston. Made up??
Cannot say whether he is handsome or not
Six foot tall? Six foot two? Which is it??
Imaginary friend?

Maria had also been keeping a list of direct quotes: "He's mine," and "Just drop it about my brother," and "Shut up."

"That last one could have been about anything," Georgia had pointed out.

"Noted." Maria had drawn a line through that one.

Now, on their way to the glass house, Roly told them what had happened. Winslow had gone through Roly's private, personal stuff.

"Exactly what private, personal stuff?" Maria asked.

"All my stuff's in a heavy-duty trash bag under my bed," he said. Now they'd reached the end of Belmont Street, and they crossed over to the field beyond which the pines grew. "And Winslow Farley opened it up and rooted around in there with his grubby little raccoon hands, and he found that recording of my ma reading a bedtime story." Roly bent double to pick up a sword-length stick and whacked the dry, scrubby weeds and grass with it as he walked. "And he played it on Mr. Farley's stupid"—*whack*—"old"—*whack*—"computer!"

Georgia shifted Freddy to her other shoulder. She remembered Roly telling them about that CD. She'd imagined having a recording like that with her mother's voice speaking to her, only her, and answering some of Georgia's questions: *Of course I love you! I wanted to take you with me. I love you to the moon and back.* But—wait a second—hadn't he . . .

"Stop right there!" Maria put her hand out. "Gimme

that stick; you're driving me crazy." Roly handed it over. "You told us you were too old for bedtime stories, remember?" Maria snapped the stick over her knee. "You told us you threw that CD in the garbage."

Roly stared Maria right in the eyes for what seemed like a long time. Beads of sweat popped out on his forehead. It was pretty hot in the field, but still. His mouth wiggled around as if his lips were fighting with each other. "*Well . . . ,*" he finally began, low voiced. "*I . . . ,*" he said, "*didn't!*"

"Innnnteresting." Maria tossed the sticks aside, and they all started walking again. Georgia felt some raindrops plop onto her arm just as they entered the cover of the woods, where she put Freddy down to walk awhile on his leash.

"So then what happened?" Maria wanted to know.

"I smacked him upside the head," said Roly, "which he deserved, the little brat."

Georgia and Freddy fell quickly behind, and so she called to the others to hold up. Freddy's pace was so slow as to be basically standing still while he poked around the ground. Raindrops plopped down around them, but gently, their fall interrupted by leaves and branches.

"He should never have gone through my personal and private stuff," said Roly, still on the subject of

Winslow's rottenness. "That stuff is none of his business. It's *my* business. Mine."

Georgia found a couple Chiclets in her pocket and fished them out.

"Boy, you wouldn't last a day around my house," Maria said. Georgia handed one Chiclet to Maria and the other one to Roly.

Roly popped the gum in his mouth. He chomped and chomped. "You know the worst part?" he said.

"Chiclets lose their flavor so fast?" Maria said.

"The worst part," said Roly, "was the look on Winslow's face." He swallowed his gum with an obvious gulp.

Maria pushed up her glasses. "That gum will stay in your liver for ten years, you know."

Roly went on as if he didn't care one bit about his liver. "He looked . . . "

"Hurt?" Maria suggested. "Mad? Traumatized? Stricken?"

He nodded slowly. "Stricken."

"That's because you struck him."

Roly shoved his fists in his pockets and frowned at his feet. "I made him lose heart."

Lose heart—the way Roly said those words, it sounded as if to lose heart was to suffer the world's cruelest fate. The words hung in the air around the trees. Had that happened to her? Slowly, Georgia put her hand to her heart. She couldn't feel it beating. Had she lost heart when Blythe left with Lyle Lenczycki? Had she lost heart a little each day ever since?

Georgia bent to pick up Freddy from the ground. But Blythe was back now—BIB!—and her heart was not in danger anymore.

Maria poked Roly's arm. "Well? What happened after that?"

Roly shrugged and started walking, and Georgia and Maria fell into step with him. "Oh, he told on me," he said, "and I got a lecture straight out of—somewhere—the Book of Brimstone or something." He ran a hand over his head. His red hair stuck out all over, and so did his ears. "I had to say sorry for smacking Winslow, and Winslow had to say sorry for messing with my stuff and playing the CD. And then by suppertime he was all smiles and big . . . goofy teeth and stupid jokes like it never even happened. Like he'd forgotten all about it."

Georgia doubted that Winslow had forgotten.

Roly broke off a twig from a bush he brushed by. "Mrs. Farley made us clean up after supper, just us two. After that she made us play nice—we played Go Fish and Old Maid for an *hour*."

Go Fish and Old Maid were very boring games.

Roland tossed the twig to the ground. "And *then* I threw that CD in the garbage."

The rain was really coming down by the time they got to the railroad tracks. There was no fear of trains running them over; trains didn't run along the track during the day. *Not till after rush hour*, went the local joke in a town with no traffic lights. But still they dashed across the tracks, because it was only smart to do so. Plus here they were out in the open and they were getting soaked.

They ran the rest of the way, through the rain, and when they got to the glass house, Georgia went in first, scouting for a safe place to set Freddy down. At first he just stood there with his thorned head up and his sturdy legs planted and the scales of his throat puffed out. After a moment of playing statue, he waved one foot and stepped carefully from Georgia's side. He dipped his triangle head to the ground.

"I hope the bugs out here in the wild aren't bad for him," said Maria. She was wringing the water from a rope of black hair. Roly was squeezing out the hem of his T-shirt.

"Me too," said Georgia. Although after the hissing

cockroaches, any bugs around here would probably be a delicious step up.

Roly shook his head like a wet dog, and Georgia ducked from the spray. Something was different. Maria and Roly had made changes. In the living room, there was a metal folding chair and a box for a footstool. Beside the chair there was a wooden crate on its end, serving as a table for a bunch of wildflowers in a canning jar. Georgia recognized some of the flowers—bachelor's buttons, Queen Anne's lace, and yellow brown-eyed Susans—from her dad's guide to *Wildflowers of the Northern Realm.* There was a stack of magazines in the bottom of the crate.

Whistling, Georgia poked at the arrangement, moving the flowers around in the jar. She realized she was covering up for a feeling. Maybe she was a tiny bit jealous that her friends had come to the glass house without her. But why wouldn't they? She'd been off having fun with Blythe. Were they supposed to stop everything and wait for her? She stopped whistling. "It looks really nice in here," she said. It really did. She sat in the chair and crossed her arms. "Comfy!" She lifted her feet and landed them heavily on the footstool.

"Don't!" Roly shouted at the same time Maria said, "What's that box?" Georgia drew back her feet and scooched to the edge of the seat.

Roly got a pleased and clever look on his face, and knelt to open the box. "Kaboom!" he said.

Maria and Georgia leaned in close to see. Then they jumped back as if the box were full of dynamite.

"*¡Ay Dios mío!*" Maria peered again into the box.

"I like to blow stuff up," Roly said.

The box was full of fireworks! They were labeled in shocking purples and pinks and red, white, and blue, with names like poppers and snaps; parachutes and spinners; fountains and Roman candles. There were ones with flower names—peony and dahlia—which made Georgia think of Blythe in her daffodil dress.

Maria pointed firmly at the box. "Georgia? We have to pretend we never saw what's in there."

"What are you *talking* about?" Roly said.

Maria put her hands on her hips. "Fireworks are illegal, Roland!"

"No, sir," said Roly. "Everybody shoots off fireworks."

"The *fire* department shoots off fireworks, sponsored by Maine Central Power, and everybody else does sparklers. Where'd you get 'em, anyway?" said Maria.

Roly crossed his arms. "A guy."

"A guy?" said Maria.

"A guy I know."

"What guy you know?"

Roly hiked up his shoulders, hands out, palms up. "A guy selling fireworks!"

"Well, it *is* illegal—maybe you were not aware—but I'm telling you, in the state of Maine you can't set those off, no way." Maria shook her head. "No way, no how. You better not be caught with those whatsoever. Like my *abuela* always says"—she looked up; the rain had stopped—"it's fun till someone loses an eye."

The sun found its way through the vine-covered gable of the house and down to the floor, where it made a small, bright leaf of light. It shimmered. They all looked at the patch of sun on the flagstone. "It looks like the opening to another land," murmured Maria.

Then, as if the pattern of sun had made its own noise, Georgia heard something go *snap*.

Chapter 11

Georgia scooped up Freddy and whipped around and saw something out of the corner of her eye.

"It's a wood fairy," whispered Maria as she slipped her notebook out of her flowered tote.

"I hope it's not a skunk," whispered Georgia, stroking Freddy's back. He was probably afraid of skunks. *She* sure was.

"It's a weasel," said Roland.

Oh no—

Then Roly jumped up and waved his arms and yelled, and Freddy's beard puffed out, and Roly yelled some more, and then: "Show yourself, you weasel!"

Winslow Farley crawled out from behind a pricker bush.

"I was following you the whole time!" Winslow stood and brushed off his shorts. "I'm very good at being quiet." He took a few sneaky steps into the glass house on tiptoes to demonstrate his skill.

Roly said, "This is our hideout, not yours!"

"I want to hide out too!" said Winslow.

"From what?" Roly threw his hands wide. "Your parents who treat you like a little *prince*?"

"What, ho, another prince!" said Maria. "You are most welcome here, dear cousin," she said, with the bowing-deeply-hand-to-heart business.

"What's so fun?" Winslow said. "What's fun till somebody loses an eye? You were saying that before. What were you talking about? Lemme see what's in the box!"

Roly grabbed two fistfuls of his own hair and went, "Gahh!"

"Oh, all the things we do," Maria said, ignoring Roly. "Lawn darts, nighttime capture the flag—just all fun in general, and *fireworks* in *particular*."

Roly wasn't convinced. "Any dope can light off fireworks," he said. "You just light the fuse"—he pretended to thumb a cigarette lighter, *pfft-tshh*—"and run like crazy."

Maria put her hands on her hips. "I guess you didn't

live here when Skip Thibodeau lost a hand."

Roly stared at Maria. "He did not."

"He certainly did," Maria said.

"Not by lighting off fireworks, though," Georgia said. Skippy's accident had been grounds for a lawsuit at the sawmill.

"I know, but still," Maria said, with a dark look for each of them. "It's *possible* to lose a hand."

"Oh, all right," Roly said. "Shoot, I wasted two weeks' allowance on those." He put his hands on Winslow's shoulders. "Winslow. Listen. You can't tell, you hear me? I didn't even know they were illegal, I swear. You promise?"

Winslow nodded solemnly. "I promise."

"Swear on the holy Bible?"

"I swear."

"Good." Roly's hands dropped from Winslow's thin shoulders. "Now get lost."

"You can't say get lost—I'm your brother now!"

"No, you're not. I already have a brother!"

Winslow drooped. "You do?"

"Yeah. I do," said Roly. "Your days as my fake brother are numbered."

Winslow pulled on his lip and tugged on his shorts. "What's his name?"

"Tony."

Maria frowned, flipping pages of her notebook. "You said—"

"Tony the Tiger," Roly said.

Maria rolled her eyes and quit flipping.

"That's not a real person," Winslow said. "How old is he?"

"Nearly eighteen."

"How tall is he?"

"Six foot one."

"What color hair?"

"Brown."

"Eyes?"

"Brown." Roly squeezed his eyes shut, a little shake of his head. "Blue."

Winslow was like a short, skinny detective on TV, and Roly his surly informant. Maria was really enjoying the show. She went back to writing, a big smile on her face, probably jotting new proof of the MoP.

"How come he's not here?" Winslow continued.

Roly didn't answer.

"I mean, how come he doesn't live with us too?" Winslow said.

Maria tapped her pen against her chin. "That is an excellent question, Winslow," she said.

Roly twisted in place. "He's in juvie."

"What's juvie?"

"It's jail for kids."

Winslow gasped.

Maria's tongue poked out, her glasses slipped down her nose; her pen was moving fast.

"Just—drop it about my brother," Roly said, "I don't want to talk about it!" He sealed his lips with a tight frown.

Winslow hugged himself into an even smaller shape, and Georgia putted his shoulder.

Maria clicked her pen. She squinted at Roland. "Do you *really* have a brother?"

Roly's face took on a purplish color, and he made fists that could make diamonds out of coal. "Yes!" he hollered. "What did I just *say*? Now go home, Winslow, and leave me alone."

Georgia set Freddy on the ground again. "If Winslow gets lost, you'll be in big trouble."

"He got here; he can get back."

"He was following us," Maria said, "and he's only little." She winked at Winslow to show she didn't *mean* it; she was on his side.

"Fine," Roly said. "But I don't have to talk to him." He pointed a finger to a corner of the house. "Sit over there and be quiet so I can pretend you're not here," he said to Winslow without looking at him. "Pretend you're dead."

Winslow went and sat in the corner and fussed around, sighing dramatically and fiddling with rocks; he was better at sneaking than at playing dead.

"What are you guys doing?" Winslow called from his corner.

"Making a room for Freddy," Georgia said.

"Writing a novel," Maria said.

"Ignoring you," said Roly.

Georgia went over and gave Winslow the end of Freddy's leash. "You can pet him. Just be very gentle."

"Why are you making rooms?" Winslow asked. "I wish I could take Boat out on a fish leash," he added wistfully.

"Because it's an imagination place," said Georgia. "This is the kitchen, and that one's the living room."

"*Ignore* him," Roly said.

Winslow pitched a pebble. "Baby Jesus wants us to get along," he called.

Roly raised his arm as if he might run over there and bring it down on Winslow's head. Freddy's beard puffed and darkened. Winslow flinched.

Roland let his arm drop. "I'm not going to whack

you, Winslow," he said. "Just—be quiet already, would ya?"

Winslow pitched a few more pebbles. After a while he said, "Baby Jesus would not like us crossing the railroad tracks."

"Then you shouldn't have followed us, dummy," said Roland.

"Baby Jesus would not like you calling me dummy," Winslow said.

Roly glared at Winslow. He crossed his arms over his chest. Winslow glared back. It seemed like they could both win a staring contest pretty handily.

At last, Roly blinked. "For . . . a . . . *baby*," he said, in a low voice and slowly, "*Jesus* sure has a lot of strong opinions."

Winslow's eyes grew big and round. He clapped both hands over his mouth. Then a noise slipped out.

It sounded like he might be choking.

Roly glanced nervously at Georgia, then at Maria.

Then Winslow's hands came away like a cork popping, and he bubbled with laughter. He toppled sideways and rolled on the ground, holding his stomach. Freddy raised one foot and seemed to be pointing at Winslow.

"I'm—I'm gonna throw up!" Winslow squealed, giggling.

"Do not throw up!" Roly hollered. "No throwing up in the clubhouse!"

Georgia and Maria started laughing too. Winslow was just too cute. Roly tried hard to be mad, but he couldn't keep it up. He started laughing too. They laughed and laughed, till Freddy's beard even deflated he'd gotten so used to the sound.

Later, when they came out of the pines, Winslow tugged on Roly's T-shirt. "I won't tell Mommy what you said."

"Okay," said Roly, "and I won't tell her you're a sneaky weasel."

Winslow nodded gravely. "I won't tell her about *you-know-what*."

"Yep," said Roly.

"The fireworks, and what you said about Baby Jesus."

Roly looked at Winslow for a long moment.

"Thanks." Roly reached out a hand and ruffled the curls on the top of Winslow's head.

This time Winslow didn't even flinch.

Georgia scratched Freddy's head. He didn't flinch either.

Chapter 12

When she got home, Georgia settled Freddy into his tank for the night. He seemed very contented from his day at the glass house. At least, he closed his eyes and sort of glowed. Then she dashed down the stairs and out the door and grabbed her bike to ride to Belmont Street. Her dad was on evening shift, so she was to have dinner and another sleepover with Blythe and Rosie.

She pedaled straight down Garden Street, turned right onto Main; she waved to Patty van Winkle, who was closing up the Pet Stop. The air was like a swamp— hot and humid—and clouds were gathering again. It was the kind of summer day that would end in a thunderstorm. She hoped it would, anyway; a late rain would cool things off for sleeping that night. She turned right on Belmont, rode by Ms. Bennett, the school librarian, out for a run with her dog, Booksie, and coasted to a stop in the driveway. Georgia put down the kickstand and took off her helmet. Wet with sweat, her hair stuck to her forehead. Georgia loved a good summer storm. There was nothing more thrilling than the crack of lightning and the rumble of thunder; nothing more shivery than counting one-Mississippi, two-Mississippi to calculate the closeness of the storm, the possibility of a lightning strike, when you're cozy and safe inside a screened-in porch.

Georgia set her helmet down just inside the door, whistling all the while. For once, Georgia was whistling out of actual happiness! She wasn't pretending to be happy when she wasn't. She'd had a fun day with her friends, and Freddy had really taken to being in the glass house! And now the thought of getting to feed Rosie her dinner and change her diaper and give her a bath and put her to bed made her chest go buzzy with anticipation, just exactly like a Christmas morning.

"Somebody's happy," said Blythe.

An edge to Blythe's voice made Georgia instantly cautious. An edge, and at the same time a looseness. Blythe was sitting at the bar-top island, and a blender full of something frothy sat on the counter. She leaned back, her legs crossed in a relaxed posture, but the foot of her crossed leg went kick. Kick. Rosie fussed in her bouncy chair on the floor.

Blythe sipped from a glass of the frothy stuff, swallowed. Looking at the glass, she said, "Where've you been?"

Georgia licked her dry lips. "I—with Roly and Maria," she said, "and Winslow, actual—"

"I thought you were helping me with dinner."

"I am!" Georgia's eyes darted around the kitchen. "Aren't I?"

Blythe uncrossed her legs, swiveled the stool, and planted her hands on her thighs, taking a long look at the clock on the stove. Georgia followed her movements: the time read five thirty. Blythe pushed against the counter to swivel back to Georgia. Narrowed her eyes. "You're late."

"It's only—"

Blythe tilted her head—slight, sharp—crossed her legs. Kicked.

Georgia swallowed. "I thought—"

"You thought!"

"I didn't know—"

"You didn't know!"

Georgia's mouth was dry. What was going on? What was wrong here? Georgia knelt to get Rosie out of the bouncy chair—and to break Blythe's icy stare. The Velcro straps made a ripping sound.

Blythe's foot stopped kicking. She hiked her shoulders and let them drop, relaxed, and smiled as if—yes, as if nothing was going on, nothing was wrong. "I just wish you wouldn't stay away all day like that, is all." Blythe's voice was lighter now, but Georgia still sensed an edge. She stood up, adjusting Rosie in her arms.

Blythe drained the contents of her tall glass and set it on the counter, where it slid a tiny bit in its own pool of water. Georgia understood that the edge, and the looseness, had to do with the frothy drink. "It's too late to make what I wanted," Blythe said, pouring what was left in the blender into the glass. "Hope you like scrambled eggs." The blender made a dull clack as she set it on the counter.

Georgia swayed, rocking Rosie, and pointed at the blender. "What is it?"

"This?" Blythe cocked the glass. "Piña colada. It's a rum drink. Rummy-yummy. It's what they drink in ex-o-*tic* ports of call." Blythe uncrossed her legs and held out the glass to Georgia. "Here," she said. "Try it."

Georgia hiked Rosie up on her hip, then took the

drink. The glass was cold in her hand and slick against her lips.

Blythe was looking at her. "Sweetheart," she said; her voice was very light now, light as air. "If you don't want to spend time with me, maybe I should just"—she shrugged and looked away—"leave."

The drink went down cold in Georgia's throat. It was sweet, and it burned, and it landed in her stomach like a fist.

Blythe hopped down off the bar stool and put her arms out for Rosemary. "You make the eggs while I set the table."

"Mom—"

"We need some music around here!" Blythe danced her way into the living room, navigating around the baby swing that hung in the doorway. Georgia stood there, feet cemented to the floor, glass dripping in her hand, cold.

Georgia didn't feel quite inside her body as she made the scrambled eggs. Sitting at the table, she felt like she was floating near the ceiling, looking down. She ate the eggs but didn't taste them. Blythe talked and ate and smacked her lips, and Rosie babbled and made a mess of her high chair tray.

Blythe wiped her lips with her napkin. "Delicious!" she said. "The cheese and chives—genius!" She raised her glass—she was drinking wine now. "To the chef!" Georgia raised her wineglass of lemonade. Their glasses clinked, and Blythe winked and said, "Chin-chin!" It sounded so familiar—the clink, the chin-chin cheers. Georgia remembered these sounds from before, when they were a family—Blythe and Stan and Georgia—eating dinner around the table on Garden Street. Flowers in a vase, pretty plates. *Clink-clink*; chin-chin. She could hear them in her head, these sounds, like an echo.

"Ooh, I just remembered!" Blythe said, hopping up from the table. "Wait here!" She went down the hall and came back with a shopping bag. She pushed aside the eggy plates and put the bag on the table. "Open it!"

Georgia stood so she could look inside the shopping bag. Inside was tissue paper, and inside the tissue paper were three dresses. Each one was different in size and style, but all three were made from the same yellow-flowered material.

"One for me, one for you, and a baby dress for Rosie!"

Georgia held the dress up to her body and looked down at it. "Mom . . ." She lowered the dress and sat back down. She felt heavy. "What did you mean before? What did you mean—about leaving again?"

Blythe looked confused for a second. Then, "Oh, *that*," she said, waving a dismissive hand. "Nothing, Georgie, I didn't mean what I said." She leaned forward in her chair and put a hand on Georgia's thigh. "I was just being silly. How could I ever leave?"

Georgia pulled her lips inside her teeth and looked at Blythe from under her eyebrows.

"Okay, I get it, ha-ha," Blythe said. She rolled her eyes and leaned back in her chair. "How could I ever leave *again*?" She pushed back her chair and stood up, gesturing to Georgia. "Come here," she said.

Georgia stood up, the yellow dress crumpled in her hands. Blythe pulled her into a hug that pinned her fists to her stomach.

It seemed like a game. A guessing game. Guess the meaning from the clues . . . the dress, the lemonade.

She could smell alcohol, feel Blythe's warm breath on her ear whispering, "I got you." Blythe rocked Georgia side to side, then let her go. "I'll get these." She flung a hand toward the table, the dirty dishes, the sink. "I'll get 'em in the morning—let's go and watch the storm."

They went out onto the screened-in porch. Georgia hoped Freddy wasn't afraid at home. They saw the jagged lightning—one-Mississipi . . . two-Mississippi—and waited for the thunder.

Chapter 13

The next day was the Fourth of July. By nine a.m. the parade was in full swing. Blythe and Georgia sat together in lawn chairs at the corner of Garden Street across from the green, where they had a good view of the parade as it wove its way up State Street and turned the corner onto Main. Rosie babbled in her stroller underneath a yellow sun hat. They all wore the new matching yellow dresses.

Across the street, the Farleys had taken up a spot on the green. Roly and Winslow were standing with their heads together while Mr. Farley aimed a camera at them. As Georgia watched, Roly said something and then said some more with his hands, and then Winslow doubled over and laughed. Winslow looked like a very real brother, at the moment, no matter how much Roly denied it.

Georgia's stomach ached with the queasy remains of yesterday. After the storm had passed, they'd put Rosie to bed and watched TV. Blythe fell asleep before the end of the show, so Georgia covered her with a blanket and turned off the TV and went to bed and had dreams that got away when she woke to the smell of breakfast. Blythe made pancakes in funny animal shapes. There was no edge to Blythe's voice; no whiff of last night's weirdness.

They watched the antique cars roll slowly by, sponsored by Mike's Affordable Tire and Brake. Then the Rotarians, the Kiwanians, the Lions, the Shriners, the Moose Lodge, and the Elks.

Sometimes Georgia's worry machine kicked on for no good reason. Maybe there'd been nothing last night; nothing wrong at all—just some scrambled eggs, a passing summer storm.

"Georgia, here's a question: Would you rather watch a parade, or be *in* the parade?"

"I don't know," Georgia said. "Both are good."

"No, you have to choose—one or the other."

Georgia thought about it as she watched Patty van Winkle maneuver a corner, leading twenty-five or so dogs and their people. They kept running around so it was hard to keep count. Patty's ten-week spring-summer obedience class always culminated in the Pets on Parade entry. Some of the dogs were better behaved than others.

Blythe tickled Georgia's neck, and Georgia squirmed. "Come on, play my game!"

TexTrax, the place where Maria's dad worked, had an actual float. Martin was driving the truck that pulled the trailer, both hands gripping the steering wheel. Georgia waved to Mr. Garcia on the float, and he waved back.

"Bzzzt! Time's up!" Blythe said. "There's no wrong answer, Georgia. It's just a game."

Georgia twisted in her lawn chair. She felt sure there was always a wrong answer and a right answer.

"Oh, never mind," Blythe said. "I'm just having fun with you."

"Which would *you* choose?" Georgia said. She had a feeling she'd disappointed her mom.

"*In* the parade, no question," Blythe said. She waved like royalty, elbow-elbow, wrist-wrist, looking left and right. "Hello, goodbye! Hello, goodbye!" she said in a proper British voice, and Georgia giggled. She peeked under the bonnet of the stroller to look at Rosie. Fast asleep, even with a parade marching by.

They clapped extra hard for the Sardine School

kids, with their bright patchwork banner and the col-
lages they'd made to show the places they lived in the
other seasons of the year. Mrs. Garcia marched along,
one hand holding Maya's, the other holding Marisol's,
and carrying Matilda in a front pack. "How much you
want to bet she can rub her belly and chew gum at the
same time?" Blythe said, and waved and shouted "Hal-
loooo!" at Maria's mom.

Georgia spotted Maria herding some of the little
kids. "Maria!"

"Georgia!"

"Phantom! Phanny!"

A huge smoky Great Dane came loping against
parade traffic, dangling a leash. Phanny must have broken rank with the Pets on Parade group. "That nick-
name lacks the dignity called for by the breed," said
Blythe. They watched the big dog run happily away.
"Go, dog, go!" Blythe said. Then she turned to Georgia.

"Don't we all look pretty in our dresses? We'll have to
get a family picture when Lyle gets back." She squeezed
Georgia's arm. "I'm so happy!" she said. "We're having
so much fun together!"

The Prospect Harbor High School Blue Lobsters
marching band came blaring by with snare drums and
trumpets and flutes. The parade slowed suddenly but the

trumpet section wasn't paying attention and bumped into the trombones. Mr. Schmottlach, the band director, shouted at the line—"Pick it up! Street beat four!"— but everybody was laughing too much to play. Georgia peeked again at Rosie. She couldn't believe Rosie was sleeping through all this drumming and honking!

"And Lyle is wonderful, you'll see!" Blythe shouted now, to be heard over the sounds of Sousa. "I can't wait for him to get back so you can get to know him!" she yelled. "To know him is to love him!"

Georgia grinned and nodded while saying in her mind a little prayer about Lyle's appendix.

A clown with a big red frown painted over his mouth and extending down his jowls—a single tear inked onto his white-painted cheeks—flopped over to Georgia in his big black shoes and handed her a tiny red rosette. The sad clown smiled; the impression was confusing.

Blythe leaned close. "Move in with us!" A bullhorn in Georgia's ear. She pulled back and looked at Georgia expectantly, smiling, eyebrows raised. Sweat stuck to curls of her hair against the bluish skin of her temples.

"On Belmont Street? But what about Dad?"

Blythe said, "You'll see him plenty, and besides, you're over at our house most of the time anyway! We'll just make it official!"

"What about Freddy?"

"Yes! Freddy!" Blythe said, and she clapped and nodded.

The sound of the Blue Lobsters band was fading. Here came the employees of the plant with their banner: HARMON LOBSTER: THE PRIDE OF DOWN EAST MAINE. Georgia searched the group for her dad. Then she pictured Florence Deonn's handwritten schedule on the fridge under the lobster magnet—and remembered he was at work till five. Holiday pay. She caught sight of Florence's big flowered Sunday church hat, and under it, Florence's brown face, shiny-damp from the heat despite the shade of the hat and the flapping of a paper fan. "Yoo-hoo, I see you, Georgia!" Florence shouted, waving at her with the fan.

"Hey, Florence!"

How would her dad feel about it? She didn't want him to be sad. Would he be sad? She figured he would. She pictured him in his pajamas, playing solitaire. It was so *quiet* there, tick-tock, tick-tock. On Belmont Street, there was music and candles and cut flowers in a vase . . . and there was Rosie, above all else.

Georgia clapped half-heartedly for the Bike Brigade—a bunch of bikes decorated with crepe paper streamers. The baseball cards clothespinned to the spokes clacked. Basically any kid who wanted to be in the parade but wasn't in any particular club could join the Bike Brigade. Winslow brought up the rear, riding a tricycle, his skinny little legs pedaling as fast as he could go. He still didn't know how to ride a bike; "I need a big brother to teach me," he'd said. Whined, really, but Georgia couldn't blame him. It was just sad, a seven-year-old on a trike.

And what about *Lyle*? Lyle was spending the long holiday weekend with his mother in Rhode Island. But he would return, he wouldn't stay away forever, and then what? Did she really want to be under the same roof as Lyle Lenczycki? To know him was to *not* love him, she was sure of *that*.

If a mirror rolled by right now, Georgia was pretty sure her face would look like that clown's, wearing a huge smile and a painted-on frown. Or was it a frown with the smile painted on? It was hard to tell. She didn't know what to do or how to choose.

"Well?" said Blythe. "What do you say?"

"I said I had to think about it."

They'd gone to the glass house after the parade.

Maria leaned back in the chair and pushed up her glasses. "Okay. Let's review. On the one hand, you've got Stanley Weathers: strong and silent. Lets you win at board games."

"He does not!"

"Do you often win?"

Georgia frowned.

"Mm*hmm*. Moving on. He cooks interesting food. He knows a little about a lot of things. He doesn't judge."

"He doesn't really *talk*!"

"Well, then he doesn't say anything judgy, does he, and therefore, as far as we can tell, he doesn't judge!"

Georgia thought about it. Maybe he was considerate. Maybe he was listening.

"Okay, then there's Blythe. Tons of fun. Beautiful singing voice. You missed her when she was gone. She's your mom, plain and simple. I'd be miserable without my mom; I'll say it. But then again, my dad's pretty great too. I'd also be miserable without *him*."

"They moved out of the house, Maria; they left you!" said Roly.

Maria waved a hand and shook her head. "Nah, they didn't *leave* us, they just leave us alone. It's good! Why do you think Martin got his license as soon as legally possible? Because nobody would drive us around! And me and Martin and Miguel are all *astounding* babysitters— ask anybody. We know baby CPR. Plus, how do you think

I learned to cook my signature shrimp Scampi? Get it? Shrimp *Scamp*-i? Because, the Scamp?" Maria arched an eyebrow. "Because we have to fend for ourselves all summer. We figure it out."

Roly sat down on the flagstone floor. "You're very *mature* about this," he said.

Maria snorted. "Yeah, well. The truth is, my *abuela* told us to quit complaining and appreciate the fact we get to rule the world all summer." Maria mimed puffing on a cigarette. "*Dios mío, chiquitos*—count blessings, not grievances." Maria flicked the ash from the pretend cigarette and shrugged. "Plus, I can read in bed as long as I want!"

"This isn't really helping me decide what to do," Georgia said. She sat down on the ground too. Then she stretched out flat and flopped her arms and legs like a rag doll.

"Okay," said Maria. "Let's think about motive."

Georgia got up on one elbow. "This isn't your novel, Maria, it's my *life*!"

Maria had started writing a book titled *The Dragon in the Glass Castle: A Novel of Romance and Suspense*. "I know," Maria said, "but still. What's Blythe's motive in asking you to move in?"

Roly dropped his head in his hands, as if the whole thing was tiring him out.

"Well—she loves me and wants us to be a family—her, me, Rosie . . . and Lyle." Georgia sat up and tugged at a weed growing between the stones.

"Right. But you don't want anything to do with Lyle; you've made that super crystal clear."

"Yeah . . ."

"What's the biggest reason to move to Belmont Street?

"Rosie."

"What's the biggest reason *not* to move to Belmont?"

"Dad."

"What's the only thing in the middle?

"Lyle."

"Stop with all the questions!" Roly said, lifting his head. "I can't hear myself think!"

"Oh, you're thinking?"

"Yes, I'm thinking!"

"Because you look like you're taking a nap!"

Georgia sighed. "I just keep wishing it would all go back to how it was before Lyle ever showed up and my parents were happy and Blythe had never left in the first place and I was just like Rosemary: not a care in the world." She dug a pebble out of the dirt. But . . . then again . . . if Lyle had never showed up and taken Blythe away, then there would *be* no Rosie. Rosie wouldn't exist in all the world. She shivered off the sickening thought. "But I can't have Blythe and Rosie without Lyle Lenczycki." She chucked the pebble. "His appendix is perfectly fine."

"Huh?"

"Never mind," said Georgia morosely. "I want to move to Belmont Street, mostly because of Rosie. But if I move in with them, doesn't it seem like I'm giving up on my parents ever getting back together?"

"Lyle messed everything up, is what you're saying," Roly said. "I get that." Roly punched a fist into his other hand with more gusto than Georgia would have expected. "He messed everything up." *Punch*. Georgia was touched that Roly seemed to care so much about her situation.

Maria leaned forward in the chair. "Any foe of yours is a foe of mine." A crafty look came over her face. "Actually, this is perfect," she said, her voice rising with excitement. "In a novel of suspense, you would keep your enemy close." Maria made her eyes big. "Definitely move in with them. *Infiltrate*."

"Infiltrate?"

"Definitely! You can do your machinations from the inside."

"Machinations?"

"Ahh, machinations," Roly said, nodding

"Let me think." Maria pulled on her chin. "You could constantly talk about your dad's many outstanding qualities? He has a good job at Harmon Lobster."

"He's a line lead," Georgia said.

"That's good solid work that'll never go away," Maria said. "That's money in the bank right there, a job in the lobster business. He cooks. He's a student of life! A jack-of-all-trades!" Maria was remembering all the aspects of the Stanley Weathers character analysis without even having to check her notes. "He always knows the right thing to say, and he says it with the greatest economy."

Georgia said, "I guess . . ."

"Or I know!" Maria stabbed the air. "Attack from the other side! You can point out the shaky nature of *Lyle's* line of business. He's always on the road, always staying at shady motels . . . what is he *doing*?"

"He's in sales?"

Maria narrowed her eyes. "What exactly does he *sell*? Do we even really know?"

"Health food."

"Sounds fishy. Check it out."

"This will never work," Roly said.

Maria pointed straight at him. "Hey! Truth is stranger than fiction, Roly; it'll work." She turned to Georgia. "Listen. Here's the secret plan: Move into the house on Belmont. Go all in; bring Freddy."

"I'll do it," Georgia said.

Maria nodded, satisfied. "All will be revealed," she said. "Trust the process."

Chapter 14

Now it was evening at Georgia's father's house.
"Gather up anything you need or want!"
Blythe had told her. Anything as long as it
wasn't Freddy. It seemed like Blythe was going back
on her word. But had Georgia only *thought* Blythe
had said she wanted Freddy to come along? "I love
Freddy!" is how she had started to say no. "But . . .
it's just . . . I don't want him in my *house,* per se. A big
lizard. And his creepy-crawly food. No thank *ew*." She
pinched her nose.

Georgia didn't want to leave Freddy behind, but it was
only temporary. Now that she had a secret plan, it probably wouldn't be long before they'd all be together, plus
Freddy, minus Lyle. So here they were in Georgia's room

so that she could show Stan how to take care of Freddy.

Blythe leaned against the doorjamb, arms crossed. Georgia and Stan stood side by side, leaning over Freddy's tank.

"So this tells you the basic things." Georgia handed Stan the *The Care and Keeping of Your Bearded Dragon* pamphlet. Freddy was hiding partly under the rock, in the sand. Did he look a little sick?

"I'll study it," Stan said.

"Okay. Just remember, don't wiggle your fingers at him. He doesn't like that."

"Okay. No wiggling fingers."

"And you scoop him up with the palm of your hand, like this." Georgia made a slow, scooping motion with her hand. "Oh, and before you pick him up, just wait till he's ready. If he closes his eyes and sort of blinks, like this?" She closed her eyes, blinked. "Then you can pick him up. But slowly! Don't hover."

"No hovering."

"And if his beard goes dark? That means he's mad, so you should leave him alone."

"Okay. I'll give him some room if he's mad."

"And if his belly gets cool when he's been out of the tank for a while, that means it's time to put him back. He doesn't like to get cold."

"Okay."

"Oh, and see? He's shedding his skin. It comes off in bits and pieces."

"Okay. Bits and pieces."

"Not all at once like a snake does. It's normal. Oh, and look, he'll wave to you. See?" Freddy had raised the front leg that was visible. "See how it looks like he's waving?"

"Hello, Freddy," Stan said. "Hello."

Blythe made a noise, behind them. "Yes, well, good-bye now, Freddy."

Georgia and Stan both turned their heads and looked at her over their shoulders. Then they both straightened up.

Georgia put her finger on the note taped to the glass—*Give Freddy a Better Life*—then dropped her hand and looked away. "Just—pet him very gently."

"Gently," Stan said. "I promise."

They went downstairs. "Blythe, can I talk to you a minute?" Stan rubbed the back of his head with one hand. He still held the *Care and Keeping* pamphlet in the other. "In the other room?"

Georgia tried to catch her father's eye. She looked pointedly at him. She made her eyes big, raised her eyebrows, nodded slowly. She was trying to tell him, without using words, the nature of the secret plan. In response he scowled, frowned, and shook his head. He was not hearing what she was saying with her eyes. All the better; he'd learn all about the secret plan once it worked! She smiled even bigger, opened her eyes wider, and nodded some more.

He looked like he was about to say something, but then Blythe cut in. "Stanley, your hair. You look like Wolfman Stan."

He pointed the pamphlet down the hall, the way a parking lot attendant directs cars. "I only need a minute," he said.

"Oh, come on, Stan," Blythe said. "Anything you want to say to me you can say in front of her; we have no secrets here."

No secrets here? Georgia snickered, thinking of the secret plan, and they both looked at her sharply. She shrugged and smiled and lifted her eyebrows and rocked a little on her heels, like a person who was not being tricky— like someone whose worry machine was parked in the garage! They both tipped their heads at her like a pair of lovebirds on a wire, then went back to glaring at each other.

Georgia's dad slipped the pamphlet in his chest pocket, then tightened his apron strings at Blythe. "Indulge me," he said.

Blythe followed him down the hallway to the den. He opened the door for her, and when she passed through, their hands nearly brushed. The door closed behind them. Seeing them walk down the hall together, Georgia could remember when they used to hold hands. All three of them, Georgia in the middle! They'd lift her between them and swing her as they walked. It would take so little—nothing at all—for them to take each other's hands again.

Maybe they were holding hands right now! Georgia moved down the hall, closer to the closed door. She heard her father talking loudly.

It was unusual to hear Stanley Weathers raise his voice. That was a good quality right there, an even temper. Georgia made a mental note. She moved closer to the door. Having a secret plan was making her sort of reckless. Even with her ear against the door she caught only snippets—her dad's voice loud, her mother's a buttery murmur. *Abandon . . . broke her heart . . . how could . . . letters . . . when it suits you . . . push away . . .*

Georgia didn't want to get caught eavesdropping. She hurried back to the other room. They were arguing—about *her* in some way—and that made her feel important. But—and this made her happy—they wouldn't *have* to argue once Lyle was out of the picture. She smiled to herself and picked up a deck of cards from the table. Idly she started sorting the deck into suits. Then she gave up on that and shuffled them instead. Shuffle, shuffle, shuffle the cards. Shuffle, shuffle the cards.

A couple minutes later her parents came out of the den. Georgia evened the edges of the deck in her hands.

Stan walked to her and stood very close. He placed his hands on her shoulders and looked her in the eyes. "That door will always be open," he said, with a glance in the direction of the front entryway. Then he squeezed her in a bear hug that smooshed her arms against her chest and sent half the deck flying. She beamed thoughts at him: *I've got a secret plan! A secret plan! I'll make things go back to how they were before we ever heard the name Lyle Lenczycki!*

"I can't argue . . . ," her father said. "I wish . . . ," he tried again. He pulled back and held her at arm's length. "It's important for you to be with your baby sister," he managed at last. He bent to pick up the playing cards.

"That's exactly what mom said!" Georgia's hands came together over her heart. See? They were all thinking the same way; they were all on the same page!

He squared the deck and placed it on the table. "Rosemary should get to see how terrific her big sister is. How very lucky she is to have such a . . ." His voice trailed. He swallowed, and stabbed at his eyes with a corner of his apron. "Such a good kid in her life."

He hugged her one more time, and Georgia whispered, "Don't worry, Dad." When he let her go, she winked.

At Belmont Street, Georgia learned how to get Rosemary in and out of her high chair, how to feed her with a little rubber-tipped spoon, how to clean her little hands. When Georgia changed her diaper, Rosie drooled, smiling up from the changing table.

Oh my aching heart, Georgia thought. She's better than a lizard.

"It's sure nice of Dad to take care of Freddy," she said, and glanced over at Blythe where she sat in the glider chair. "Stanley Weathers has many times been named employee of the month at Harmon Lobster. Many times. He is a highly responsible person."

"Mmhmm. Highly." Blythe was flipping through a magazine with a sailboat on the front.

Georgia shivered with happiness. It was obviously working. Blythe was remembering all the good qualities.

"All done, Rosie-toes," Georgia said. Rosemary waved her little hands in the air, trying to reach Georgia's face. Georgia leaned slowly closer, closer, closer to Rosie, and as she did, Rosie's eyes grew even larger, and her mouth made an O. Then she smiled with her four tiny teeth, and she patted Georgia's cheeks. She patted them a little harder, making Georgia blink. Then she pinched them. Georgia didn't think she could even pull away from those teeny, tiny, pinchy little fingers. It was like getting a massage from an owl. The whole pinchy thing clearly delighted Rosie, because she chortled and kicked her legs in the air like a frog.

Georgia had probably, in spite of the actual pain, never experienced a happier moment in her life. "You know who loves babies is *Dad*," she said.

"Mmhmm." Blythe smiled a little—she agreed!—and went back to her travel magazine. She was thinking warm thoughts, Georgia could tell.

"Geeg," went Rosie.

"Did she just say my name?"

Blythe shrugged, smiling. "Maybe!"

Okay, *this* was the happiest moment of her life.

The phone rang. Blythe got up. The magazine flapped to the floor.

It was for Georgia. "Your first phone call in your new home!" Blythe said, clapping. Georgia set Rosie on her blankie on the floor and went for the phone.

"All is going according to *plahn*?" Maria was using a spy voice, which sounded vaguely German.

Georgia looked over her shoulder. She had laid the groundwork. Lyle would be back tomorrow. And if things continued the way they were going, there would probably be some bad news for poor ol' Lyle Lenczycki.

Georgia cupped a hand over her mouth and spoke— spylike—into the phone. "All is going according to *plahn*."

Chapter 15

When Lyle arrived home from his business trip late Sunday afternoon, he went from Traveling-Salesman Model to Man-Cooking-Supper Model with a quick change of clothes. Lyle didn't have a beard, but he looked like he could grow one overnight. When he ran a hand through his hair it fell thickly and perfectly back into place. His eyes crinkled naturally with his smile, which was easy and dazzling as he moved effortlessly around the kitchen, making small talk, asking about everybody's day.

What a jerk.

Now Lyle was peeking into the oven, where a chocolate cake was cooking while "Wheels on the Bus" blared rinky-dinkily from the speakers in the other room.

Blythe was sitting at the island counter on a bar stool, bouncing Rosemary on her lap and flipping through a magazine. And Rosemary was crying.

Blythe moaned. "Georgia, take the baby," she said over Rosie's wailing. "I'm getting one of my headaches."

Funny—Georgia remembered the headaches only now; she wondered how they could have slipped her mind. When Blythe used to get her headaches, there was no piano playing. No dance parties or singing. Blythe would withdraw to her bedroom, leaving Georgia and her dad alone, sometimes for days.

Georgia shook herself to try to line up the sudden flash of memory with the Blythe here and now in the kitchen. It was as if there were pieces of Memory-Blythe and pieces of Now-Blythe . . . and Georgia's brain was a kaleidoscope seeing the pieces all at once, the shifting shapes and colors.

Lyle's deep voice snapped off the kaleidoscope. "You go and take a lie-down till dinner's ready, okay?" He wiped his hands on his apron and massaged Blythe's shoulders, then leaned to kiss her cheek. "I promise a feast to cure a headache of any size. Even Blythe-size."

Blythe looked up at him and smiled wanly, patting his hand. "Thank you, Lyle. I'm so glad you're home.

You're a prince among men." She glanced wearily at Georgia. "A saint among stepfathers."

"Well!" said Lyle to Georgia after Blythe disappeared through the swinging door and down the hall beyond. "Who wants to lick the bowl?" He set the bowl on the counter near Georgia and put out his arms for Rosemary.

The bowl had a good amount of batter clinging to the sides. A generous amount. Even though her mouth watered, Georgia didn't touch it. She wasn't falling for any of his traps.

Right away, Rosie quit fussing. Lyle tossed her above his head just a little; caught her and held her close. She cackled. That was the word for it. Then Lyle started to sing along to the music coming from the living room. Badly. He raised his eyebrows as if to invite Georgia to sing along.

"*Old MacDonald had a farm . . . ,*" he sang, off-key.

"*Eee-i-ee-i-oh,*" Georgia joined in—for Rosie's delight only—but when Lyle's face lit up as if she'd given him a gift, just by singing with him, she stopped. His teeth were very bright. Like a row of perfect light bulbs. Maybe he could chomp them and swallow the glass. She shuddered—that one went too far; the appendix had been about right.

"Old MacDonald had a farm!" he sang, alone now. *"And on this farm he had some pigs!"*

Rosie was clapping her little hands. Georgia wanted to sing too—sing for Rosie—but she didn't want to make Lyle think she was on his side in any way. Because she wasn't.

"With an oink-oink here and an oink-oink there—"

"Could you *please* keep it down?" came Blythe's distant call.

"Oops!" Lyle put his forehead to Rosie's and whispered "Shhh." Rosie's chortle was surprisingly loud and deep, coming as it was from a baby. Lyle strode into the living room—avoiding the baby swing that hung from the doorframe—and shortly the music stopped. Stepping back into the kitchen, he maneuvered Rosie into the baby swing. Rosie observed in rapture the movement of her own bare feet.

Lyle picked up the bowl, making no comment about the fact that Georgia had ignored it. Keeping his hurt feelings to himself, she figured. He fumbled the batter bowl; it slipped and clattered on the floor. "Oops again!"

Good. Maybe he wasn't perfect, despite his perfect hair and his perfectly fashionable clothes and his perfectly healthy *appendix*. Maybe he was actually a clumsy idiot. Georgia could only hope.

"Here's when we need a dog, right?" Lyle said, disappearing behind the bar-top island to pick up the bowl. "A dog would clean this up in a jiffy!"

"Dogs aren't supposed to eat chocolate," Georgia said in a flat voice.

"Oh gosh!" Lyle popped back up like a jack-in-the-box. "See? I need someone like you to protect innocent pets from me!"

Georgia said, "Onions too."

"Oh, good grief! I need you to protect poor innocent onions from me too?" said Lyle.

Georgia rolled her eyes. Rudely, she hoped. "I *mean*, onions are poison to dogs."

"Wow. I'm glad you told me that, for the next time I chop onions around a dog." There! Sarcasm! She was getting on his nerves for sure. Lyle smiled. His eyes crinkled. Maybe not sarcasm, then. She couldn't be sure.

He pulled a package of chicken from the fridge. Quietly, absently, he hummed the music that wasn't playing anymore. *"With a hmm-hmm here, and a hmm-hmm there . . . ,"* he sang.

Rosemary bounced in the baby swing. Drooling, she jammed her little fist in her mouth and happily gnawed on it. Georgia sang softly, bending to gently clap Rosie's tender little feet. She couldn't help it. *"Woof-woof, here, woof-woof there* . . . are you my little puppy, Rosie-toes?" Georgia figured Lyle would join in the second she started singing, but he didn't; he let her be. When she glanced at him, he was focused on the chicken.

It was nice in the kitchen now that Lyle had dropped the friendly stepfather act for five seconds. The evening light came in the windows, softening all the edges. Rosie gurgled in her baby swing. Nothing heavy hung in the silence, and she didn't feel her usual desperate need to fill it the way she did at home. At *home*-home, on Garden Street. Lyle, chopping parsley, smiled. Georgia smiled too, before she knew what she was doing. Then she turned her back on him. She didn't want to make that mistake again.

Georgia pushed Rosie in the baby swing. Back and forth. Rosie gurgled. The noises behind her—the dishes' gentle *clank* and *clink*, the *shoop* and *thud* of the knife cutting vegetables on a wooden board—reminded her that at home, her father was probably heating up a Dandy Diner dinner, the ones they kept in the freezer for emergencies, while she was here on Belmont Street and soon to be served fancy chicken on a pretty plate.

"So, how do you know so much about chocolate and onions, Georgia?" Lyle said behind her. "Do you have a dog at home?"

"Nope," Georgia said. Rosemary began to fuss a little in the swing in the doorway. Georgia gave her a gentle push.

"I never had a dog," Lyle was saying to the homey *thunk* of wooden spoon, the gentle close of a cupboard. "When I was a boy, I had a pet coral snake named Chelsea."

Maybe her dad wasn't even bothering to eat back at home without her. Maybe he was feeling alone and left out because people were doing important things without him. Rosie swung forward and back. That way and this way.

That door will always be open. He'd seemed sad. Georgia felt guilty for moving in here. But she did it for them! For Mom and Dad! It was all part of the secret plan!

"She was a good snake," Lyle said. She still didn't turn around. She heard the click of gas flame, the rasp of a pan on a burner. "And very beautiful, too, not that that's the important thing."

Bang-rackety-clacker!

Georgia turned—Lyle had dropped a colander. He raised his shoulders—*eek*—and with a glance at the swinging door put his finger to his lips—*shhh!*— and retrieved the colander from the floor. Then he wiped his hands on a kitchen towel and tossed it on his shoulder, just the way her dad always did.

If it weren't for Lyle Lenczycki, Mr. Nearly Perfect, Georgia wouldn't be here feeling terrible. It wasn't her fault she'd moved out—it was Lyle's fault. And clearly Lyle was a tough nut to crack. All that . . . *niceness*. She gave Rosie another push, sending her a little higher in the swing. Lyle was the one who drove Blythe away in his new blue car and left Georgia and her dad alone, with the quiet and the clock and the cowboy lasagna.

"Did my mom tell you how she gave me Freddy?" Georgia said. She kept her back turned.

"Freddy?"

"My bearded dragon," Georgia said. It felt like she'd left part of herself on Garden Street, in Freddy.

"Oh, right!"

"My dad is taking care of him at our house."

"You know, Georgia, I'm very interested in bearded dragons and in all kinds of reptiles, actually, ever since Chelsea came into my life and wrapped herself like a scarf around my neck. Of course, one day she went *out* of my life . . ."

It was getting very hot in the kitchen now, with the oven baking and the flame on under the pan.

"Do you like chicken kiev?" Lyle asked.

As if she'd ever eaten chicken kiev. She turned around and faced him. "Freddy eats live cockroaches," she said, just to gross him out.

"Cackakaka!" Rosie yelled.

"Can you keep it down out there, *please*?" came Blythe's voice.

Lyle put a finger to his lips. "Hey! Here's an idea," he said softly. He pointed toward the living room. "If we move the couch over, that would make room for a tank—a home-away-from-home for Fred—"

"No!" Georgia said sharply.

"Oh." Lyle pulled back, clutching the dish towel. "Of course," he said. "I didn't mean to—"

"Mom gave me Freddy the day she left." Georgia narrowed her eyes. "With you."

"Oh," said Lyle. "Yes." He frowned and smiled a little, as if he didn't know which one to settle on, considering. "I see."

The oven timer dinged. The cake was done.

"My *father* loves Freddy," Georgia said, "and he takes good care of him." Not to mention Blythe had already said no to having Freddy here.

"Of course," said Lyle. "Of course he does. I understand."

No, you do not understand, thought Georgia. You

don't understand a single thing. Conversation over. *Parfait.*

Georgia wrestled Rosemary out of her swing and carried her into the living room and left Lyle standing there with the timer dinging.

"Can somebody turn that off?" came Blythe's faint cry.

Georgia plopped down on the couch and bounced Rosie on her lap. After a moment, she heard the oven door open and close, the sound of the pans sliding on the racks. The chocolate cake smelled good, but she wasn't hungry. She wouldn't eat it.

If only Lyle had never come along. Why didn't he stay in Blythe's past, where he belonged? Then everything would be how it was before. Stan would stop inventing terrible casseroles. He'd *talk*, maybe. Didn't he talk before? If Georgia had forgotten Blythe's headaches, what else had she mixed up in her brain? If Blythe would only come back home, Blythe would cook wonderful food—she loved to cook, didn't she?—and the piano wouldn't be gathering dust. That's where the piano was, after all, at *home*, not here on dumb Belmont Street. If Blythe came home, she'd play Georgia to sleep every night, and greet her every morning with a song.

Rosie grabbed a hank of Georgia's hair and tugged.

Without Lyle, there would be no Rosie; Georgia knew that. But now he could go. Nobody needed him here. Why couldn't it be Blythe and Dad and her and Rosie and Freddy? Why couldn't that be her family?

If only Lyle Lenczycki would go away on his next sales trip and never come back.

Chapter 16

On Friday it was hot, hot, hot. Damp air clung to the skin, and dark clouds hung heavy beyond the steeple of the Voice of the Trumpet church. The Farleys were finally hosting the long-threatened holy potluck and they'd invited Georgia and Maria—even though supposedly the reason Roly had made friends with them was so this potluck would never take place.

"What a scam," said Roly.

There were three swings in the church's little playground, and Georgia and Maria and Roly were sitting on them. Maria's *rabona* filled and deflated a little each time she swung back and forth. Georgia wore a sundress. They'd thought it was a dress-up occasion, but it wasn't: Roly's sweat plastered that same old keep KEEP

ON TRUCKIN' shirt to his back. Didn't he have any other shirts?

"I like this one!" Roly said when asked.

Nearby on the grass of the green, Blythe and Mrs. Farley and Mrs. Garcia were sitting on a blanket with Rosie and Maria's three sisters. Georgia had a happy thought that the little girls would grow up to be friends.

Over on the blacktop parking lot, Lyle Lenczycki was under the basketball hoop playing a pickup game with Maria's dad and her brothers Martin and Miguel, and Ms. Bennett, who, though not tall, had deadly aim. Lyle caught a pass from Mr. Garcia, took a shot. The basketball sailed high over the backboard.

"Not even close," said Maria.

"Nope," said Georgia.

Maria plucked at a thread of her skirt and looked broodingly at her brothers. "Those two are going to do something unchurchical, I just know it."

Now Mrs. Farley clapped her hands and started gathering the Sunday school kids. As soon as she'd gotten a few together, a couple others wandered off. Martin and Miguel sauntered over from the basketball game and hung around the swing set.

"Why are you guys loitering?" Maria said. "You weren't even invited!"

"Everyone welcome," Martin said solemnly as Miguel pointed a long arm at the church sign: VOICE OF THE TRUMPET: EVERYONE WELCOME.

After a brief staring contest, Maria said, "Well, it's a *potluck*; you know what a potluck is?"

Martin looked wounded. "Of course we know what a potluck is, Maria."

"We're not heathens," said Miguel.

They both pointed to the long table of waiting food—Mrs. Farley's sheet cake, Mrs. Garcia's enchiladas, Lyle's pasta primavera—and a jumbo bag of Jet-Puffed marshmallows.

"That's just wrong," said Maria.

Maria's brothers high-fived each other, shouting "Marshmallows!" and "Marshmallows for the win!"

"It's not a *contest*—oh, forget it," said Maria.

"Attention, everyone!" Mrs. Farley called. "Come over here, Roly!"

Roly pushed off the swing and they watched him go and stand where she told him to stand. He looked like he was going before a firing squad.

"Praise him with trumpet sound!" shouted Mrs. Farley. "Praise him with lute and harp! Praise him with tambourine and dance; praise him with strings and pipe! Praise him with loud! Clashing! Cymbals!"

"Well, *that's* a teensy bit over the top . . . ," Maria muttered to Georgia.

"Praise the Lord!" said Mrs. Farley.

"Ah. I guess she doesn't mean *Roly*," Maria whispered.

"And so, Roland Park," Mrs. Farley went on, "the children of Voice of the Trumpet Ministry have prepared a special song." She scooped her hands in the air, which had the effect of bunching the Sunday school kids like bananas. "All together now!" cried Mrs. Farley. They began to sing:

> *"Roland, you are welcome here.*
> *God and children hold you dear!"*

Georgia recognized the tune as something close to "Wheels on the Bus."

> *"Hear the trumpet, lift your heart,*
> *Now you're here, we'll never part."*

The second verse was the same as the first, only with choreography. Winslow sang the loudest. At the end they all linked arms and glowed as if lit by halos. Everybody applauded. Roly covered his face with his hands.

After the song, there were games. Winslow and his friend Jason came in second in the three-legged race. As they crossed the finish line Winslow yelled, "Look, Roly! Hey, Roly, I won sec—" and promptly whomped to the ground, taking Jason with him.

Roly shook his head and chewed on a piece of grass.

Then there was an endless game of tag. Winslow kept running over to the swing set where Roly was sitting it out, tagging him—"You're it! You're it!"—and scampering away. Roly never moved an inch from the swing. "Calling it *toilet tag* makes it even worse," he said, watching the kids running around and squatting. "Maybe it's just me."

"Absolutely"; "Definitely worse," Georgia and Maria said at the same time.

Later, Winslow hollered, "Hey, Roly, watch me, watch me!" Roly squinted over at the Sunday school kids playing H.O.R.S.E. on the blacktop, and waggled his fingers near his cheek, a mockery of a wave. Winslow bent double and then heaved the ball underhand toward the basket with all his might. It bounced to the blacktop a good six feet short. His face fell. Roly gave a slow clap.

"He's just trying to impress you," Maria said.

Roly kicked the dirt under the swing and sent up a puff of dust. "I'm not impressed."

"Come on, it's nice." Georgia forked some of Lyle's pasta primavera from her paper plate. "And the song?"

"Stupid." Roly scowled. "It was *too* nice."

"What's that supposed to mean?" Maria rested her plate in her lap and reached for her notebook.

"It means—sure, they're nice *now*, but that only means they can take it away later," Roly said. "The niceness."

"They're not going to take it away," Maria said.

"How do *you* know?" Roly said.

"Because they're actually nice!"

Georgia rubbed her forehead and thought of Lyle.

"Yeah. Well. I'm taking *myself* away, so—" Roly shrugged. "So they should just . . . quit being so nice all the time."

Now they watched Winslow and a couple other kids build a tower on the grass using shoe-box-size brick-patterned blocks from the Sunday school playroom. Every time Winslow piled on another block, he looked to see if Roly was watching. "Hey, Roly!" Winslow's giggles and squeals made Georgia think of Rosie, and how much she loved her already. How she would do anything for her. How she couldn't stand it if Rosie got taken away. It was true, what Roly said. Important things—people—can go away. Disappear. She'd known that since the fourth grade.

Winslow put another brick on the tower—it was taller than him now—and hopped up and down. "Roly, Roly, Roly!" he said.

Roly dropped his plate of enchiladas on the ground, got up, squared his shoulders, and strode across the grass to the tower. Winslow grinned. Roly opened his arms as if he was going to hug Winslow or pat him on the back or something. Instead he swung wide and flat-handed the whole thing over.

"What'd you do *that* for?" Winslow wailed. Mrs. Farley hustled over and bent close to Roly, saying something only he could hear, while at the same time comforting Winslow with a tender hand on the back of his neck. Roly pulled away and stormed off across the blacktop.

Maria took a big bite of pasta, shaking her head as she chewed and swallowed. "Speaking of behaving badly, how's the secret plan working? Was family supper a disaster as planned?"

Georgia looked out over the green, at the people on picnic blankets. "It was a disaster, all right."

Blythe had emerged from her bedroom feeling better. "My Blythe-size headache is gone now, gone and forgotten!" she'd said joyfully. The chicken kiev had been good, Georgia had to admit it. She learned that chicken kiev was chicken pounded thin and rolled around herbed butter, and then baked. It was fancy-restaurant-good. The chicken kiev was so good, in fact, that at the thought of it her mouth watered now against her will—it was so good she could *spit*! Lyle had put on some album called *Peace, Love, Ukulele*, which put everyone in a good mood, whether Georgia liked it or not. It was all in some way irresistible, as if her heart were beating, blood pumping along to the gentle, cheery ukulele music. There was nothing she could do about her heart beating and her blood pumping, right?

Around the supper table, Lyle had launched a spelling bee with unusual words—*chilblains*, *gangrene*—and Georgia won the bee on *abecedarius* without even knowing what it meant! And although she had staunchly vowed, in the hours before, not to eat Lyle's chocolate cake, she had not been able to keep that promise. The cake was delicious. Ugh! She could spit *again*! Finally, after supper, Blythe had announced it was the "golden hour" and herded them to the backyard, where they'd stood for a family picture in front of a fancy camera set up on a tripod. They put on their matching yellow dresses, and Lyle changed into a new yellow shirt. "Say *chee-ese*!" Lyle sang out. Georgia tried not to say it; she tried not to smile. But then Rosemary wiggled and went "gheeyeeyee" and that was that. It was probably the best family picture ever taken in the history of family pictures.

"Disappointing," Maria said when Georgia was done. She took out her notebook, shaking her head. "This is very bad."

Later, Winslow brought over another plate of food for Roly, but Roly didn't touch it. He would only eat marshmallows.

"See?" said Martin. "We told you marshmallows would win the potluck."

Chapter 17

That night, Georgia collapsed into bed and fell asleep with her clothes on. She dreamed she was wandering the woods in the dark.

In the dream, she came to a glass house. Why was it there? What was it for? Why was nobody using it? Why had it been abandoned?

There was only the slightest warning—a small sound, like a wind chime, a flicker of light—before it happened. A rain of glass. Shards cut her skin; some cut deep, others pricked like pins. The shattering was terrible and beautiful—unreal colors, pops and fizzes of sound; there was a strange joy, being inside the kaleidoscopic rain of glass and color and sound, inside and outside both, watching and experiencing at the same time.

Dream Georgia saw a second box of fireworks. She could light them off. She could hide them. She could keep them. She could give them away. She could turn them in at the police or the fire station. A book appeared, then opened, printed with tiny letters she couldn't make out, but still she knew what the words said: "Then the Lord commanded the fish!"

Baby Rosie was there—had she been there all along? She was in her baby swing suspended from—from what?— and the shattered glass and colors were still raining down around them, endlessly. Rosie's skin was too soft and pink. Georgia yanked her T-shirt off over her head and covered Rosie with it. Then Georgia was bare to the shattered night.

Morning. But still night. She was hot from sleep, and thirsty. She went downstairs to the kitchen for some juice, and was surprised first to smell coffee, then to see her mother there, sitting at the island on a bar stool.

"Oh, good, you're up," Blythe said as if it wasn't— Georgia looked at the clock on the stove—5:07 a.m. "Georgia, let's talk." Blythe seemed jumpy, as if she'd already drunk the whole pot of coffee.

Georgia's dream lingered around her like a mist.

Something about Roly's fireworks, the box hidden in the glass house.

"Tell me, Georgia." Blythe looked sharply at Georgia. "Tell me your dreams."

Huh! Blythe could see the mist. Georgia yawned, rubbed her eyes. "Well, I was walking in the dark woods, and then there was a wind chime, and then all of a sudden there was . . ."

Blythe was making a *no-no-no* face . . .

"Shattered—"

. . . and shaking her head. "Not your *dreams*; I mean"—she reached for the coffee pot, poured—"your *dreams*." She sat back in the bar stool, hands wrapped around the mug. "What do you want to do, to *be*?"

It was so early. Lyle and Rosie were still asleep. Georgia yawned again and pulled at the damp neck of her shirt. She couldn't think of anything.

Blythe sipped birdlike from the mug, peering, waiting. "Come on, you must have *some* dream. You and I are alike that way."

We are? thought Georgia.

"We have dreams!" Blythe clicked her fingernails along the side of the mug. "Play my game, Georgia. What's your dream? The sky's the limit."

"I—" Georgia's mouth was dry. "I dream . . ." She

hadn't actually gotten that juice. "I want to be an astro-naut."

Blythe's eyes opened wide. Blank. Then she threw her head back and laughed.

Georgia's answer must not have been enough; it was the biggest thing she could think of. The dream mist was all gone now; her body had gone cold. She thought Lyle and Rosie might wake up from the noise of the laughter.

Blythe finally stopped laughing her head off. "Oh, that is perfect!" She took a napkin and dabbed her eyes, and now her face said *my-my-my*. "I just love that." She was done with the laughing and wiping her eyes, and now she leaned her forearms on the counter and said, "Okay, your turn."

Georgia didn't understand.

"My game, silly, come on! Now you ask me what *my* dream is."

The bright eyes, the early hour, the sharp voice—Georgia hesitated. She licked her dry lips. "What is your dream?"

Blythe pushed back from the counter. She looked over each shoulder before continuing, as if she had a secret for Georgia alone. "I have received a thrilling job offer," she said, softly now, "or very near one, anyway, on Elegance Cruise Lines!" Her face was so bright.

"Oh!" Georgia said. Wait. A cruise line? On the ocean?

"Mostly hostessing in the dining rooms—but singing, Thursday nights! There's a ballroom, and a stage with spotlights." Blythe fanned her fingers; *imagine that!*

Georgia's stomach was a cold stone. Yes, she could imagine the ballroom . . . on a ship . . . a ship bearing her mother away.

Chapter 18

Not again. Not again, no! Georgia tried to say something—anything. "Mom—"

But Blythe just kept on talking, as if her leaving—*leaving*!—was nothing but great news and happy chatter. "It's like Las Vegas, only better! It's like New York City on the high seas! My dream come true!"

Georgia's hands went to her clammy cheeks. She felt floaty, as if she were rising out of her body. She wanted *Lyle* to go away, not *Blythe*. She'd done it wrong—she must have. Somehow this must be her fault; she just didn't know how. "That's—your dream?"

"Well, no—but yes! Singing, piano, making people happy, meeting new and interesting people all the time, and—oh honey, look at your face, that *face*!" Blythe tilted her head and tucked her chin; her lifted brows and pulled-in lips meant: *Wait*; *there's more.* "Georgia. Listen. Here's the best part." Blythe leaned closer. "If I get the job—it isn't a sure thing just yet, I won't know for sure for another couple weeks—but assuming I get the job . . ." She looked up from under her lashes. "You're coming with me! You and Rosie both!"

Georgia didn't understand. Blythe clapped and gave a little squeal. "We'll homeschool; we'll *boat*-school! And we'll see the world! At least the run from Cape Liberty to Montreal," she said as she pulled a brochure from her bathrobe pocket and unfolded it on the counter. "Eleven days at a pop, Georgie, look at this." Georgia tried to follow Blythe's finger as it traced the route. The words on the map didn't make sense in her brain. Newport, Bay of Fundy, Nova Scotia, Halifax.

"I can see you in an astronaut suit already, honey," Blythe said, looking into the distance and fanning her fingers again: *the stage, the lights*. "And you know"— she pointed at Georgia—"there's no better place to make those important connections than onboard an expensive cruise ship. Those fancy NASA people all take cruises. Trust me." Blythe put her hands flat on the counter. "What do you think?"

Georgia had to look away from Blythe's urgent

face; she caught the time on the stove from the corner of her eye. 5:13 a.m. They'd been talking only six minutes. Outside it was still dark, but inside everything had changed.

Just then, upstairs, Rosie started crying. Georgia's head flashed with the remnants of her bad dream—the splinters of glass, the importance of Rosie's soft skin. They could hear Lyle's feet hit the floor; footsteps.

Blythe grabbed Georgia's wrist. "Don't tell," she said. "Keep it secret till I've really got the job. Don't tell anybody—don't tell Stan; you'll jinx it." She let go. "Your father had you all to himself while I barely laid eyes on you." The huffy way she said it, Georgia wondered if she'd forgot who'd been the one to disappear. Blythe smiled big and hugged herself. "So," she said. "What do you think, are you happy?" She cocked an ear toward the sound of Lyle's footsteps on the stairs. "*Shhh*, tell me quick."

"I think," Georgia whispered, "it's whacktastic." She looked at Blythe and hoped it was enough.

Chapter 19

The next days passed uneventfully, but Georgia's worry machine wouldn't shut off. Blythe said it was as good as "a done deal," but that talking about it before she'd officially been hired would jinx it and ruin the whole wonderful thing. She promised that as soon as she got final word from Elegance Cruise Lines, they'd work it all out with Stan and Lyle and the homeschool people. But until the moment she "signed on the dotted line," Georgia was not to speak of it with anyone, not even—"especially not even!"—her father or Maria, and that was hard.

The idea of leaving with Blythe was thrilling. She felt wanted and loved—now she *knew* Blythe would never leave. Well, she would leave, but not without Georgia. Not this time.

Georgia wrote in her journal to hold her excitement—words and phrases like *whacktastic* and *dreams* and *I will see the world*.

And when she thought about leaving people behind, and about leaving Freddy behind, she pushed the thoughts way down inside.

It was late.

Lyle was away again on a sales trip, this time to upstate New York, and Blythe had gone out around four o'clock in the afternoon. Now it was nearly ten, and she hadn't come home.

Georgia couldn't very well call her father. He was working a night shift at the plant. Should she call the Garcias?

She grabbed the phone and punched the number before she could talk herself out of it. Someone picked up after the second ring.

First there was some prolonged coughing, then a clearing of the throat. "Hola."

"Lita?"

"Georgie? Is that you?"

"My mom—she's—is it okay to call this late?"

"Eh, you know how it is. Everybody's out back by the Scamp, poking the fire, doing a drum circle or something. It's all fun and games till someone loses an eye. Now. What's this about; what's going on?"

"Well . . ." Rosemary was upstairs, peacefully asleep. Everything was actually fine, wasn't it? Rosie was fed and dry, and when she'd cried, Georgia had rocked her, murmuring, *I got you . . . I got you*, over and over. Everything was fine. Georgia was probably being dumb.

"Spit it out," Lita said helpfully.

Georgia took a deep breath. "It's just that Blythe left at four and she said she'd be home by supper and I made spaghetti but now it's—" Georgia looked at the things on the table—the salt, the bowl, the candle, the bottle. "The spaghetti's cold, it's all . . . clumped—"

"We're coming over."

"You got oil and eggs around here, Georgie?"

Maria and Lita were there. Maria's parents were out looking for Blythe.

"I think so," said Georgia.

Lita pulled a box of Kitchen D'light brownie mix out of her handbag, and a jar of raspberry jam, and directed the girls to bake a pan of brownies with jam stripes.

Maria frowned. "What good will that do?"

"It will do *me* good."

Maria rolled her eyes.

"Whaaat? I am in the mood for brownies." Lita winked at Georgia.

The brownies were cooling on the counter when Mr. and Mrs. Garcia returned with Blythe. Georgia stood pressed against the fridge and watched her mother plop into a chair at the table. Blythe's head jerked as her gaze moved around the table: spaghetti, salt, bottle. With a sickness in her stomach, Georgia remembered that moment she first saw Rosie, how her baby head had jounced around from thing to thing till her eyes met Georgia's and stayed. Now Blythe looked at Georgia— empty smile, empty eyes. Her lipstick had all worn off, and her yellow dress was dark with sweat. *Who are you?*

"Looks like all's well here." Blythe shut her eyes and shook her head as if to clear it. "Looks like my services are not re ... re ..."

"Required?" said Lita in a voice full of lemon juice.

Blythe dipped her chin and pointed up. "Not needed."

"You could not be more wrong," said Lita.

"Ma! You're not helping." Mrs. Garcia looked pale and tired; she swiped at a lock of her hair with her wrist. "Marla, get Mrs. Lenczycki a big glass of water. Really big. Blythe, don't those brownies smell good? Georgia, why don't you cut up that pan and we'll have a nearly midnight snack, okay?"

Georgia couldn't feel the spatula in her hands.

Blythe planted her feet, leaned forward, and grabbed the wine bottle and tried to twist off the cork; made a pouty face and clunked it back on the table, where it teetered beside the wineglass. Georgia caught it, righted it, glanced at the ceiling; was that Rosemary fussing?

"Look at me, I'm as clumsy as Lyle," Blythe said. "Oops!"

"Blythe—"

"I'm as—as—appa-thetic as Stan."

Georgia's cheeks stung. The worry machine was going full blast. As *what* as Georgia? As ugly? As stupid?

"With his *picture* books."

"Field guides," Georgia said under her breath. "They're field guides."

Blythe's head looked heavy and blocky as she swiveled it toward Georgia. "I needed someone to talk to, Georgie. I don't know if he even loved me, for all he'd trouble himself to answer the"—she pressed her lips together and gathered the next word—"*question*."

"What question?"

Lita and Mrs. Garcia exchanged a look. "Let's get those shoes off, Blythe," said Mrs. Garcia.

Blythe shook off Mrs. Garcia and leaned forward, her hands on her thighs. "Do. You. Love. Me." She flung her hands—dangerously near the bottle and glass—and let them flop to her lap. "You wanna know what he said?" She sat back, flopped those hands again. "He . . . said . . . *yes.*"

"*Dios mío,*" Lita muttered.

"Of course he did! He was your husband!" Mrs. Garcia slipped a sandal from Blythe's foot and tossed it aside.

"No elaboration whatsoever. What *about* me did he love, why did he love *me*?" She was nearly shouting. Georgia listened for sounds of Rosie.

"Not now, Blythe." Mrs. Garcia tugged off the other shoe. Mr. Garcia picked up the sandals and stood there holding them as if it was an important job and someone had to do it.

Lita flapped her hands at Maria. "Quick! Another brownie for Georgie's *mami.*"

Blythe sat on her hands and swung her bare feet back and forth. Her toenail polish was pink, chipped. "*I just do,* he said. Well!" Now her hands flew high. "That was not enough for me."

Not enough, not enough, not enough. These were familiar words to Georgia, words that fueled the worry machine.

Now Georgia was sure she'd heard Rosemary fussing. She wished her mother would stop talking. Just stop. She kept her head down. Her face burned. She didn't even want to look at Maria. Maria probably was dying to write all this interesting, jot-worthy stuff down.

Blythe blathered on. "Lyle is a man from my past. Summer camp. Our eyes met. Instant bond. We were the two prettiest people at Camp Kezar pond." Blythe flung an arm—the wineglass crashed to the floor.

Rosemary started bawling.

Georgia spun and fled.

"I got you," Georgia murmured, upstairs now. Rosie's head was warm, her hair damp beneath Georgia's lips at her ear. "I got you," she said again and again, till Rosie calmed and quieted. She sat down in the glider and rocked Rosie. "Shh, shhh." She could hear the women in the kitchen—their sounds, but not their words. The clink of dishes, water from the tap. After a while, Maria came to the door of Rosie's room. Over the top of Rosie's sleepy head, Georgia put a finger to her lips. Maria nodded. She pointed to the floor, then put her hands together beside one cheek, tipped her head, closed her eyes—*sleep*. *Your mother's asleep*. Georgia understood. She gave a thumbs-up, which Maria echoed, then waved—*good night*. A few minutes later Georgia heard the front door close, and the house was completely quiet. It was only in her head that Georgia heard the sound of crashing plates.

She remembered the day Blythe left. She'd whispered to her father, "I might explode." It had been a terrible feeling. Scary. "I might explode into a million, zillion pieces." She thought he'd say, *You won't explode*, or *Don't worry*, or *You'll feel better after a good night's sleep*.

Instead, he'd nodded gravely. "I understand," he'd said. "Would it help, do you think—" he'd started to say. "Would it help if you could break something? Something outside of yourself?"

Something not my heart, Georgia thought now, remembering. Something not *his* heart, she supposed.

From a cupboard, Georgia had picked her mother's second-favorite plate. Not her first-favorite among the collection of mismatched china—Blythe would want to eat from that one when she returned. Her father chose one too. He made Georgia put on a pair of sunglasses to protect her eyes, and then they'd shattered those plates on the kitchen floor.

Did it help? It was thrilling; it was loud; it was naughty. Thinking about it now, what helped was that he'd asked, had tried, had stayed. And when she got up the morning after, she'd found him sleeping on the floor outside her room.

Georgia got up early, changed Rosie's wet, heavy diaper, and dressed her, and was feeding her squash from a tiny jar and a rubber-tipped spoon when Blythe shuffled into the kitchen in her bathrobe.

"I won't be doing that again anytime soon," Blythe said. She poured a cup of coffee from the pot that Georgia had made. "Visiting the Copper Penny, catching up with old acquaintances." She squinted at the windows, then shuffled over and pulled down a shade to block the morning sun. "No, ma'am! My poor, aching head." She shuffled over and cupped Georgia's chin—"You sleep okay?"—and then kissed her on the cheek. Her breath smelled bad.

That's it? Did she sleep okay? There was no mention of what Blythe had looked like when Maria's parents brought her home. What she'd acted like, how she'd woken Rosie with her noise. No mention of the things she'd said out loud about Georgia's dad, and about Lyle.

"It was kind of a rough night, right?" Georgia said.

"*I'll* say." Blythe laughed as if something were funny.

Chapter 20

Around lunchtime, Georgia and Maria stopped in at the Pet Stop. Roly was behind the counter and Patty van Winkle was nowhere in sight.

In the four days since the holy potluck, Roly had packed in a whole lot of troublemaking. His deeds ranged from thoughtless—tracking in mud on the wall-to-wall carpet—to mean, like knocking over Winslow's cardboard-brick tower; to alarming—he'd stayed out all night long at the glass house and the Farleys had nearly called the police. "I fell asleep!" he'd explained. "Arrest me!" And then, Patty van Winkle had caught him stealing. As punishment, she'd given him a job.

Roly pulled a cleaning cloth from his smock pocket, drew a couple lazy circles on the counter with it, and then tossed it onto his shoulder like a weary old bartender on TV. "I've seen my parents throw things," he said. "Big deal."

"She didn't *throw* it." George picked at her thumbnail. They'd been talking about what Maria termed the Night of Bittersweet Brownies. The wineglass had shattered on the kitchen floor. "She didn't mean to."

Roly whipped the rag from his shoulder and swiped at the counter again. "Maybe my parents didn't *mean* to either." Suddenly he balled up the cloth and threw it down. "But these Farleys! I'm telling you I can hardly stand it! It's awful living there."

"What's awful?" said Maria. "The Farleys? The niceness? All the food? Your own bedroom? The peace and quiet?"

"Yeah! All of that! It's not . . . real."

Maria leaned across the counter and knocked on Roly's head.

"Ow!"

"It's real, like your thick head!" she said. "You've got a good thing going here, Roly. And you've got us! *We're* here!"

Georgia's stomach churned. It felt really bad to know she was leaving, to keep secret that soon she *wouldn't* be here. Keeping the secret felt like lying. She remembered how Roly'd once said, *Friends are people who'd lie for you.* Now she was lying, all right; she was lying to her friends and to her dad. What kind of friend was that? What kind of daughter?

Jing-a-ling-a-ling!

Winslow came in carrying a brown paper bag.

"Get lost!" Roly said.

"Gentle, royal cousin, gentle," Maria said.

Winslow crept on sneaky toes to the counter and quickly set the bag on it. "Mommy-told-me-go-bring-lunch-to-your-brother-bye!" He backed away and out the door.

Jing-a-ling!

Maria lunged and knocked on Roly's head again.

"Ow! Why do you keep doing that?"

"Why do *you* keep being a big jerk?"

Roly pressed his hands to the sides of his head like he was trying to hold his brains in. "I don't *know* why, okay? I don't *know*!"

Georgia cut in. "Well, Preston's coming, right?"

Roly's hands flew out. "I know that!"

"Or so you've said a million times," Maria added. She lifted her eyebrows at Georgia and mouthed, *MoP.*

"He *is*!"

Georgia counted on her fingertips. "Only ten more days till August 1."

"Ten more days and then we'll see," said Maria.

Georgia elbowed her. "I mean, we'll *see* that everything will be *better*. Hey, why'd you do it, anyway?"

"Do what?"

"Steal the squeaky monkey."

Roly sighed, then shrugged. "Because I can," he said. "Because that's the real me. I'm good at it."

"Not *very* good at it, apparently," Maria said. "Cause you—"

"I *get* it!"

"Got caught."

Chapter 21

Roland, have you seen Winslow?" It was later that day, and the sun was nearly gone. Mrs. Farley had found Roly and Maria and Georgia on the green. Maria was writing chapter six of her book *The Dragon in the Glass Castle*, Georgia was flipping through *The Laws Guide to Drawing Birds* before dropping it in the library return slot for her dad, and Roly was trying to juggle three pine cones.

"Haven't seen him." Roly shrugged.

Mrs. Farley breathed in deep, whooshed it out. "I thought he might be with you." She looked one by one at Roly, Maria, and Georgia. "It's been so special," she said, "you all including Winslow in your adventures . . . " She fiddled with her necklace and looked around the green—church, firehouse, town hall, post office—as if Winslow might burst out the doors of one of them, or pop from behind a tree. "He's not in his room. And he's not with you, and it'll be dark soon."

"When was the last time you saw him?" Maria whipped out her notebook.

"Supper." Mrs. Farley pressed her hands together and brought them to her chin. "It's not like Winslow," she said. "Roland, did something happen between you two?"

"No! I didn't do anything!" Roly's face burned pink and he looked at the ground like he could scorch it with his eyeballs.

"All right," said Mrs. Farley. "Well—" She glanced around the green again. "If you see him . . ."

"We'll go and look for him," Georgia said.

"Thank you, Georgia," said Mrs. Farley. She took Georgia's hand in both of hers. "You're very kind."

"Ooohhh, you're very kii-iiind," Roly singsonged at Georgia as soon as Mrs. Farley was out of earshot.

A hot flare lit in Georgia's chest. "What is going on with you, lately, Roland? Quit it, okay?" She was thinking of Rosemary. "Winslow is *missing*."

"For what, a whole hour?" He tried juggling the pine cones again.

"*Fascinating*," said Maria. "*Classic.*"

Now Roly turned his angry face on Maria. "What are you talking about?"

Maria pumped her eyebrows. "I'm glad you asked!" She reached into her flowered tote and tugged out a library book: *How to Fashion Fabulous Fiction*. "I did some research on the butthead behavior you've been treating us to."

"Gee, thanks," Roly said.

Maria flipped to a page bookmarked with a coupon for toothpaste. "Listen to this."

"I don't have to listen to you," Roly said. But the pine cones remained still in his hands. He wasn't *not* listening.

"'A character behaves opposite of how he really feels,'" Maria read aloud, "'in order to divert attention from the frightening changes of situation that threaten to overturn the emotional paradigm.'" She replaced the coupon, closed the book, and dropped it into her tote. "See?" she said, adjusting her eyeglasses. "Classic."

"You think you're so smart, Maria!" He bent to pick up the pine cones from the grass at his feet.

"I *am* so smart," Maria said coolly.

"What did that even mean?"

"I'm not sure, exactly, but *this* one"—she pulled

another book from her tote, *Dynamite Characters*, and waggled it—"basically says it means you push people away before they can push *you* away."

"That's not true."

Push away . . . Georgia remembered hearing her father's voice the day she moved to Belmont Street. Those were the same words she'd overheard, *push away* . . .

"It's true, all right," Maria said. "You don't trust them with your heart, so you break *their* hearts before they can break *yours*!"

Broken heart . . . promise to stay . . . her dad's loud voice, her mother's—

"Whose hearts?"

"Theirs. Them—with a capital *T-H*. You tell me!"

"*Pfffff*. This isn't a romance novel, Maria!"

"Same applies to family *sagas*, Roland!"

Georgia's calves prickled. Her stomach roiled.

Roly pitched the pine cones hard to the ground.

"And when they don't love you, you'll think you can explain it—because you lied or stole a cat collar or a squeaky toy or stayed out too late—"

Georgia's thoughts whirled. Blythe, leaving again, together this time, though she'd promised to stay, and what about after that? Would they be on a cruise ship forever? Floating and floating away?

"—it won't just be a terrible mystery that keeps you up at night, night after night—"

"I sleep like a baby!"

Georgia squeezed her arms. She wanted them to *stop arguing*. "Stop!"

They both turned to her.

She swallowed hard, trying to calm down her mind. "Well—uh—babies don't necessarily—"

"Shut up, Georgia!"—and the two faced off again.

"Stop it!" Now Georgia's worry machine was buzzing. She squeezed her eyes shut, chanting, "Stop it, stop it, stop it, stop—"

BOOM!

Georgia's eyes flew open.

POP!

KA-BOOM!

They all turned in the direction of the sounds.

Chh-chh-chhh . . . pop-pop.

Hisssssss.

High above and far beyond the pines, the evening sky was all on fire.

Chapter 22

They pounded through the woods; never mind the scratching branches, never mind the twisty roots. *Boom*s, *pop*s, and *hiss*es from above; beneath their feet, the rumble of a train; and in the air, the smell of sulfur—fire and brimstone. They ran and ran.

The glass house.

The hidden fireworks.

Winslow.

They burst out of the woods and into the open. A sudden flare illumined the train. They had to stop at the tracks; they couldn't go any farther.

"Winslow!" Roly's cry was swallowed by the clacking, clacking, *clack-clack-clack* of the train. "Winslow!"

How long could one train be? How slowly could it move? Georgia counted cars in a whisper. Her heart banged to the beat of the cars on the track. A terrible song in her head went *Win*slow—*Win*slow—*Win*slow.

At last the caboose was in sight down the line of cars. Finally it passed.

Standing there on the other side of the tracks was Winslow. A little kid with his arms wrapped tightly around his skinny little body. Scared stiff. Then he pumped his fists in the air. "See, Roly? I still have both my hands!"

Roly took the tracks in two leaps.

"*I* set 'em off!" Winslow said. "*I* did it!"

"You idiot!" Roly got right up in front of him and Winslow shrank—hiked his shoulders, tucked his chin, squeezed his eyes shut tight.

"I'm not going to hit you, Winslow." Roly's voice shook. "I'm *never* going to hit you! We were scared!" he said. He grabbed Winslow's shoulders. "I was scared."

Winslow threw his arms around Roly's middle. "I was too."

Roly put his cheek to the top of Winslow's head— Georgia thought of Rosie's baby-fine hair—and wrapped his arms around him. After a while Maria cleared her throat.

"Did I do good?" Winslow said.

"No!" Roly pushed him to arms' length. "No, you did not do good, Winslow, you did bad." He pulled him into another long hug. "I gotta say, though . . ."

Maria narrowed her eyes. "Roly, do not encourage—"

"I'm pretty impressed," Roly said.

"Roland!" Georgia and Maria yelled at the same time.

"Totally awesome!" Roly said.

Suddenly Winslow started to cry. With relief, or that he'd done something Roly approved of, or *what*, exactly, Georgia couldn't say.

"Aww, don't cry, Win." Roly pulled him into another hug. That was three hugs! "I'm really, really, really glad you didn't lose a hand."

"Or my eye, either," Winslow said, his voice muffled inside Roly's hug.

Roly held on. "That too."

Chapter 23

The glass house was gone. Shattered. Now they were walking slowly through the woods back to town, reluctant to face Winslow's parents and whatever trouble they were in.

"I didn't even know I'd lit the whole entire box," Winslow said.

But he had. One explosive had caught the next—peony, popper, parachute—till the whole box blew.

"I didn't think I'd get out of the house in time!" Winslow said.

But he did.

"I didn't think I'd get under cover in time!" Winslow said.

He'd dived under a thicket. His only injuries were some pricker scratches.

"This was all my fault," Roly said.

"I agree," Maria said.

"The Farleys are gonna kill me," Roly said.

"They definitely are," Maria said.

"They'll kick me out before Preston gets here."

"Probably," Maria agreed.

"They'll think I'm dangerous—that I put Winslow at risk."

"You did."

"I didn't know he'd *light* them," Roly said. "Dummy."

Georgia took Winslow's hand and held it as they walked.

"But I *should* have known," Roly said after a moment.

Maria stopped short and grabbed Roly's arm. "I'm a genius!" she said. "You can come and stay at our house as long as you want! Nobody'll hardly know you're there." She started walking again, so everybody else did too. "Oh, and my parents will move back into the house when school starts up again; they always do. You could stay in the Scamp till way next June! It'll be cold in the winter, but it's better than living on the street."

Roly seemed to give the idea some thought. "Could Preston stay there too?"

Maria sighed and glanced at Georgia. "Probably. Is he very handsome?"

"What does that have to do with it?" Roly wanted to know.

"Research," Maria said. "For my romance novel."

"Yuck."

Half the town must have heard the explosion, because lots of people were gathered near the firehouse when Roly and Maria and Winslow and Georgia came out of the woods and into town. Maybe it was the fight the three of them had had about Roly's "classic" behavior. Maybe it was the danger he'd put Winslow in. Maybe it was brotherhood, or even love. Whatever the reason, when Winslow spotted his parents and ran to them, Roly didn't try to defend himself at all. Instead he begged to be forgiven.

"I'm sorry," Roly said. "I should have protected him. I'm very, awfully, totally, crazy sorry, and I don't know what else to say."

Mr. and Mrs. Farley were silent. They were speechless.

Roly lowered his head. "I know where the door is. I can see myself out."

"So to speak," said Maria; they were standing in

front of the firehouse. Maria repeated her housing offer. "Roly can come and stay with us. You know, just to head things off at the pass," she said. Mr. and Mrs. Farley still hadn't spoken a word. "To get ahead of this situation," she added. "Assuming you're going to kick him out." They seemed capable only of rocking Winslow in a jumble of arms. "To keep him off the streets."

Mrs. Farley looked like she couldn't decide whether to smack Roly or hug him. Her face kept moving around and trying to get control of itself. "Roland is not going to live on the streets, Maria," said Mrs. Farley finally.

"So that he doesn't have to sleep in the Stop & Shop dumpster, then," said Maria.

"Roland is not going to sleep in the Stop & Shop dumpster," said Mrs. Farley. Winslow finally squirmed out of his parents' group hug. "No one is going to live on the streets or sleep in a dumpster here, Maria. My word. That's a city problem."

"I slept in a dumpster one night," Roly said.

"I know, honey." Mrs. Farley glanced at Mr. Farley. "It was all in the file," she said gently, putting a hand on Roly's shoulder. "But that was away in Rumford." She smiled. "City problem."

"It could happen here."

Mrs. Farley shook her head. "Prospect Harbor is full of nice people."

"So's Rumford," said Roland. "There's even more nice people there because there's more *people*. We just happened to run out of luck. And Preston took care of me."

"Really, in a dumpster?" Maria said. She was just itching to get out her notebook, Georgia could tell.

Roly turned to Maria. "*Yes*, in a *dumpster*. Are you happy now?"

Maria smiled. "I've never been so happy in my life," she said. Then she punched him on the arm. "It sounds terrible and I feel just awful for you. Can I steal it for my novel?"

He smiled a little. "Be my guest," he said expansively.

"Thanks. I know you wouldn't give out your dumpster details to just anybody."

"When will you understand that nothing you can do will turn us away from you, Roland? Not even this. Oh, we'll be discussing it further, make no mistake, but—" Now Mrs. Farley had hold of Roly's shoulders. "Why, it says it right there in the Bible. Lord, how often will someone do something or other, and I forgive him? As many as *seven*? And Jesus says to him, I do not say to you seven times, but seventy *times* seven!" She smiled victoriously. "You see? Romans 12:19."

Winslow was doing the math under his breath.

"It's actually Matthew 18, dear," Mr. Farley murmured. "And Winslow, the number you're looking for is 490, but—it's more the spirit of the thing."

"A big number, lots of forgiveness," said Mrs. Farley, "that's the point."

"All clear!" came a shout from the firehouse. The fire truck rolled back into the station and someone shut the door of the bay. The danger had passed; nothing had caught fire. Everything was fine, they said. Everything would be fine.

Georgia felt so tired. Her legs had turned to rubber.

"We will never give up on you, Roly. We have faith in you. We have *hope* for you." Mrs. Farley really gripped Roly's shoulders now. Georgia could tell it sort of hurt, like Rosemary's pinchy fingers.

"Faith abides," Mr. Farley added. "We're all for faith. But *hope*—hope is a choice. Hope is active. We have *hope* for you, Roly."

"Well spoken, dear." Mrs. Farley let go of Roly and patted his back. "Now, then. I imagine the way you are feeling right now is punishment enough. As is the job Patty van Winkle gave you at the Pet Stop. Am I right?"

Mr. Farley nodded solemnly. "You certainly didn't mean for Winslow to come to harm, we know that."

Roly was quiet.

Georgia noticed Blythe talking to a fireman. She wondered if Lyle was home on Belmont Street with Rosie. She looked around for her dad.

"Preston stole some food from a Stop & Shop." Georgia's attention snapped to Roly. "And he got caught." Roly breathed in, breathed out. "And I ran," he said. "Mom and Dad weren't around. Dad was already in jail. Mom was 'not herself'." He made quotation marks in the air around the words. "Or maybe she was all kinds of herself. Anyhow, Preston took care of me," he said, "right up until he couldn't.'"

After a moment, Mr. Farley cleared his throat. "He sounds like a good boy. A good man."

Maria looked at Georgia, eyebrows way up, to mean: *Preston was real.*

Roly nodded, the muscles in his face tense and fighting for control. "The last thing Preston said to me in person was 'Roly, don't lose heart.'"

Winslow stuck his hand in Roly's.

Don't lose heart.

"So I'm not," said Roly.

Georgia couldn't tell if Roly squeezed the little hand in his, but he probably did.

Chapter 24

It's hard to keep a secret. Day after day, to keep keeping it.

Georgia memorized the schedule Blythe had shown her on the calendar, written with a fingertip dipped in invisible ink. Blythe would hear if she got the job no later than August 10; after that they'd take a bus and a train to Cape Liberty, New Jersey, for training ahead of departure the following Sunday.

The secret jittered inside her all the time. The jitters made it hard to know what *else* she was feeling. It would be hard to leave her dad and her friends. And Freddy. Leaving Freddy felt like leaving part of her*self* behind. She caught herself whistling a lot.

"It's not like you'll never see them again, Georgia, don't be so dramatic."

Still. It was hard to think she'd be the one to disappear.

Meanwhile, Georgia and Maria put together a going-away present for Roly. It would be inconsiderate not to; it would seem like they didn't believe Preston would come for him, even though they mostly didn't. They'd talked about it together. Preston wouldn't come; Roly wouldn't be able to say goodbye to the Farleys; he'd choose Winslow over Preston; he'd want to be a big brother instead of a little brother; it would turn out to be against the law for Preston to take Roly away; Roly would decide he didn't want to sleep in a dumpster.

"He's not going to sleep in a dumpster. Mrs. Farley said so." Georgia studied the horizon. "Don't be so dramatic."

"How does she know? She doesn't know," Maria said. "Don't be so naive."

What had Roly said the day they met? Friends are people who'd lie for you? Well, they were lying for him now. Pretending they believed him when they didn't.

Pretending they wanted his wish to come true when they didn't.

Pretending there were no secrets between them.

Somehow they'd pretended away the days, and tomorrow was August 1, and the square on the calendar at Belmont Street said *Roly Goes Away*. So they pretended they only had today in case it turned out to be true.

In the morning, Georgia and Maria made brownies with jam stripes. Even though the memory of when they'd made them before was bad—the Night of Bittersweet Brownies—the brownies were delicious, obviously. They couldn't let a bad memory spoil perfectly good brownies.

At twelve noon, they took the going-away brownies and the going-away present, and they met up with Roly and they walked through the woods and across the railroad tracks and to the clearing where the glass house had stood. They sat in the shade at the edge of the clearing and watched the shattered glass catch the sunlight—blink and wink.

"Well, here's your present," Maria said once they'd eaten all the brownies. "We wrapped it."

Roly looked the wrapping over; they'd used the funny pages from the *Rare Reminder*. Then he tore off the paper and opened the box.

He lifted the first thing from the box and undid the tissue paper.

"Recognize that?" Maria had to sit on her hands she was so excited.

It was pink—*the* pink rhinestone-studded collar he'd stolen on the day they met.

"It's for your cat," Maria said. "You want a cat, don't you?"

Roly turned the collar over in his hands. "I do want a cat."

Maria smiled triumphantly. "I knew it. And now you have the collar in advance! We paid for it and everything."

Georgia glanced at Maria. They had planned out what they would say, including the little joke about paying for the cat collar. Georgia was supposed to laugh now, so she did. It sounded fake. She wished it could be real.

Roly pulled the second present from the box and unfolded the tissue paper.

This was a stack of picture postcards—a red covered bridge, an autumn-colored tree, wildflowers, birds—ten postcards in all, and Roly turned them over, one by one. Each card had a stamp in the corner where the stamp should go. Five were addressed to Maria's post office box. And five were addressed to Georgia's.

"Wow!" said Roly. He really seemed to mean it. He could hardly take his eyes off the cards.

Maria cleared her throat—"*Ahem.*"

Georgia spoke her line. "And now, an original poem."

The first lines were Maria's.

"A boy named Roland came to town one summer day in June. Although at first he wore a frown, in time he changed his tune." She elbowed Georgia. "Now you," she whispered.

Georgia swallowed. *"He wore a T-shirt day and night. It seemed he'd just the one. He swore it was his fa-vor-ite. Its message was hard-won."*

Then it was Maria's turn again. *"'Keep on Truckin'' is what the shirt did say across the front. Please, oh please, don't do us dirt! We wish it were a stunt!"*

The last two lines they recited together.

"Now it's time to grab a tissue 'cuz we're going to really miss you."

It was quiet for a second, then Roly clapped. "That was good!"

"I know," Maria said. "It's a sonnet, a Shakespearean sonnet. 'Tissue' and 'miss you' are called a *near*-rhyme, which is better than a perfect rhyme; it's more sophisticated. We recited from memory, but don't worry," she said, "it's also written in the card." She turned to Georgia. Waited. "We made a card." Maria prompted Georgia with another jab of her elbow.

Georgia handed it over. Roly opened it and read the poem to himself; Georgia watched his lips move. He studied the school pictures they'd enclosed.

"They're wallet-size," Maria said. "For your wallet."

"Thank you," Roly said. "Thank you a lot. I don't know what else to say."

"That's enough," said Maria. "That's plenty!"

Georgia didn't know what to say either. She couldn't think of any words that would be right. Now she just wanted to go home and stop pretending he was going to leave and she wasn't.

Following Roly through the woods back to town, Georgia started to cry. Maria gripped her elbow, put her mouth to her ear, and whispered. "Don't worry, he's not even going. We just wasted a bunch of money on postcards and stamps."

Chapter 25

The next day it was August 1. They were waiting at the Handi-Mart parking lot for the evening bus due in from Rumford.

The Farleys sat with Roly on one of the benches: Mrs. Farley—Winslow—Mr. Farley—Roly. Georgia and Maria sat on the other bench. Mrs. Farley stared straight ahead. Winslow sat on his hands and swung his feet and kept glancing sidelong at Roly. Mr. Farley stared at the pinkening sky. Roly stared away up Route 1, from where the bus would come.

Georgia remembered how she'd watched out the window the day Blythe came back, how the time had gone by so slowly, and then—*boom!*—Blythe was there. And so was Lyle, and so was Rosemary, and with her father right there, too.

"I can't believe you're going," Maria said. She actually winked at Georgia.

"Believe it," said Roly. But Georgia wasn't sure he believed it either. His voice was too firm. His back was too straight. She'd listened to enough of Maria's character analyses to know the signs.

A bus appeared. They all watched as it approached, getting bigger, bigger, bigger the closer it got, and finally rolled into the Handi-Mart parking lot. Nobody moved.

The bus stopped. The door swung open. The driver stepped out and dashed to pull up the big luggage doors underneath.

One by one, the passengers got out.

"It's called debussing," Maria said. "I have never liked those kinds of words. Deplaning, debussing, detraining—don't they just sound weird?" She was chattering like a squirrel.

Georgia half expected Roly to say, "*You* sound weird," because that would be typical. But he didn't say anything. He kept his eyes on the debussing passengers; they all did. Watching and watching and watching.

They knew it was him the second they saw him because of how his face lit up; because of how Roly popped from the bench; how Mr. and Mrs. Farley rose and stood, very still, each with a hand on Winslow's shaking shoulders; and how Roland Park cried.

Georgia let out her breath and realized she'd been holding it.

"I was in the can, and I got locked in—can you believe it? I couldn't get out!" was what Preston said first. It was a nice voice. He looked a lot like Roly, only manly. He laughed. It was a nice laugh. "Maybe I'm having those psychological problems they tell you about—for when you get out."

Roly threw his arms around Preston, pinning Preston's arms to his sides. Preston's duffel bag dropped to the ground. Roly started to really blubber. Preston wormed one arm out of the tight squeeze and patted Roly's head. "You got tall," he said. Then he kissed his hair. "It's okay, Roly-poly. I'm here. Did you think for a minute I wouldn't come for you? It's okay. It's gonna be okay."

What followed were a few minutes of meeting and greeting, during which Maria was uncharacteristically pink-cheeked and silent. Mrs. Farley kindly introduced everyone—Mr. Farley, Winslow—Roly seemed incapable of speech—and Georgia and Maria. "They're my friends," Roly managed to choke out.

Preston nodded at them, smiled. "Good to meet you," he said.

"Good to meet you," Georgia and Maria said at

exactly the same time. Everybody laughed, and they elbowed each other, feeling silly.

Then there was some standing around, and then an awkward moment when the small circle holding the Farleys and the two brothers drew tighter and closed, and Georgia and Maria were outside of it. Then it seemed clear that it was time to say goodbye and leave Preston and Roly and the Farleys to whatever it was they were going to do now.

"Girls, can we give you a ride home?" Mr. Farley gestured to their minivan.

"Nah." Maria bowed and swept her arm regally. "Your carriage awaits, cousin," she said to Roly. Straightening up, she glanced at Preston and blushed like crazy.

"See you tomorrow?" Georgia said.

Roly drew his wrist under his nose and nodded. "Tomorrow."

They waved them away in the minivan. Maria took out her notebook and drew a heavy X over all the elements of the MoP.

Georgia thought again about the day Blythe left, and the day she came back. Her heart ached—that was the only word for it—at the thought of leaving herself. The way Roly had locked his arms around Preston, it looked like he was never letting go.

Chapter 26

In the morning Georgia and Maria rode their bikes past the Farleys' house just as they'd done for the first time a million years ago, and as they'd done a million times since.

On their fourth pass, Mrs. Farley came to the door, and Georgia and Maria hopped off their bikes. "He's gone," she called.

Georgia looked at Maria and back at the house. No, he couldn't be gone. That couldn't be right.

Mrs. Farley's hair was messy, as if she'd just now woken up or hadn't slept. Her face was pale, and she had dark circles under her eyes. "Winslow is beside himself!" she called. She rubbed up and down her arms as if she were cold. "Hang on," she called, and disappeared into the house.

"How could he *do* that?" Maria said, finding some words and spitting them out. She looked in disbelief at Georgia. "He really was always going to go, I guess. I thought . . . all along I thought he'd stay." Gripping the handlebars, she locked her elbows and shivered her shoulders. "I am struck dumb. I'm speechless. I have no words. I don't know what to say. I really don't." She threw her bike to the ground and plopped down onto the curb. "How could he leave without saying good-bye?"

Georgia put her kickstand down. She went and crumpled to the curb beside Maria and drew in her knees, and dropped her head onto her forearms. "Oh, Maria," she said. Her head was so heavy. "How was he supposed to say goodbye?" She was thinking about what her mother had told her that day at the lighthouse. How it broke her heart to leave, before. She was thinking, too—how was *she* supposed to say goodbye?

Georgia lifted her head with effort and sighed.

Maria wiped her nose with her sleeve. "Of *course*," she said after a minute. "Of course! Well, I can't believe it." She banged her thigh with a fist.

"I know."

"I mean I can't believe I didn't see this coming." Shaking her head, Maria reached into her flowered tote and pulled out a small packet of tissues. "It's classic," Maria said. "Rotten and awful and . . ." She tugged out a tissue and handed the packet—one last tissue remained—to Georgia. "Classic." For a little while, there were only snorts and sniffles. Sad sounds.

A single loud sob erupted from Maria. She blew her nose. "Boy, that Preston sure was handsome, though, wasn't he?"

Georgia cried a little harder.

"Let's hope we at least see *him* again," Maria said.

They were crying uncontrollably when Mrs. Farley came out of the house with a plate of cookies and a box of tissues. She plopped herself on the grass.

"Go ahead and cry, girls." She pressed her mouth hard with the back of her hand. "I was prepared for this, but even so, it's killing me, and I can't cry, for Winslow's sake."

"I've seen my mother cry," Maria wailed. "And look at me!"

They both looked at her.

"I'm very well adjusted!"

"Thank you, Maria," Mrs. Farley said. "Thank you for that." She looked at her hands in her lap. "If I'm honest, I guess I'm—I'm not feeling strong enough, just now, to cry."

Georgia's nose was running. "Where did they go? Will they come back?"

Mrs. Farley drew up her knees and wrapped her arms around them. Sitting tucked in that way, she looked much younger. "Preston had done his homework, is all I can say." She shrugged. "At least we could give him a suitcase for his things instead of that garbage bag." Slowly she shook her head, let her shoulders drop. "'And he will wipe away every tear from their eyes.' Revelations something or other."

They were all three quiet for a minute.

"I'll tell you one thing," Maria said. She yanked a tissue from the box.

"And what's that?"

Maria honked her nose. "We're gonna need a bigger box."

Chapter 27

That afternoon Georgia went to her room at her father's house to sneak some more clothes and things. "Flip-flops and a bathrobe are not going to impress the NASA people," Blythe had said about the options Georgia'd brought to Belmont Street so far.

The day crept on and on. Georgia felt flat and couldn't stop staring. Her head was full of stuffing. Her insides vibrated like bees buzzing dully.

Freddy was half-hidden in his tank. "Freddy?" He didn't move. Would he be okay without her?

Give Freddy a Better Life. Georgia peeled the old note from the side of Freddy's tank. Had she? Not if she was about to leave him behind. Georgia stroked Freddy's back with her finger. She felt very far from herself.

The note was curled and faded; she didn't tape it back onto the glass.

Later Georgia was helping Stan clean up. It had been a while since they'd eaten supper together. Her eyes smarted. She sniffed and he noticed.

Georgia blew her nose on a napkin. The glass house was gone. Roly, too, was gone, and wasn't it better for everyone that his leaving, despite all his talk of it, was in the end so sudden? Blythe had said the same about *them* leaving. Better to do it suddenly. "Trust me, I know," she'd said.

"Hey, now, hey there," her dad murmured, patting her back. She cried a little, and he put one arm around her in a side hug. The stitching on his apron bib rubbed her cheek uncomfortably. "It's sad when a friend moves away," he said. "But I bet we haven't seen the last of Roland Park."

According to the principles spelled out in *Fabulous Fiction*, Georgia should be picking a fight with her father right about now. But then again, Maria said there's always a character who behaves against formula.

Georgia pulled away and picked up the drying towel. She caught herself whistling—faking—and stopped. "Dad?"

"Mmmm?" He was rinsing the soap off the last supper dish.

"Can we play a board game?"

His face lit up. "Sure! Parcheesi? Checkers? You choose!"

"Someone's happy!" Lyle said after supper. He whistled a few bars of "Old MacDonald" with Georgia as he put his suitcase in the trunk of his car to go to the airport and board a red-eye to Arizona. This time he was heading to a national sales conference in Scottsdale, a place he'd described as being hot and with an excess of golf. "The forecast is for 105 degrees all week," he said. He slammed the trunk shut. The door popped up, and he slammed it again.

Georgia held Lyle's sports jacket over her arm. Blythe hadn't even told *Lyle* about the cruise job.

"Georgia, tell me," Blythe had said. "What does Lyle do for a living?"

"Salesman?"

"Exactly. Lyle is a *traveling* salesman. He can *tah-ravel*—ta-da!—to meet us at every port of call!" She'd smiled triumphantly. "Nothing could be easier for Lyle."

Now Georgia handed Lyle his sports jacket. "That's very hot," she said about Scottsdale.

"But it's a dry heat," Lyle explained. He smiled. "It's nice there, and I enjoy the occasional game of golf. But believe it or not, Georgia, I would rather be home with my girls, even with all this humidity." He swatted his neck. "And the mosquitoes." He looked at his palm. "Gah—missed." Then he smiled at Georgia and patted her shoulder. "I miss you more each time I go away."

My girls. Did Georgia miss Lyle when he was traveling? She couldn't quite bring herself to say it out loud, but she tried it in her mind—*I miss you too*—and it sounded real.

Blythe came out of the house with Rosie on her hip, and Lyle kissed them both goodbye. They stood in front of the house, watching the car drive away. At the corner, Lyle tooted the horn and stuck his arm out the window and waved.

"Guess what?" Blythe said, waving. "I got the job." She was still smiling and waving like a beauty pageant contestant. Then Lyle's taillights disappeared and she dropped her arm. "We leave in the morning. Everything's bumped up a week. I'll already be one day behind in my training, but I'm a quick study."

Georgia looked down the street, her heart beating fast. "But I didn't say goodbye to Lyle." His taillights were long gone.

"Yes, you did," Blythe said. "You said goodbye just now, I heard you! There's a bus to Portland, and a connection to Boston—"

"Dad and Maria—" *Bang-bang-bang* went Georgia's heart in her chest. "When did you sign the dotted line? You said as soon as you did we'd work everything out with—"

"Honey, it's late already. We have to do laundry and pack and all that. You'll tell them in the morning."

"Can I call them at least?"

"Listen to yourself! Would you want a phone call like that?" She rubbed noses with Rosemary and talked in a cute voice. "Wouldn't that make you feel weewy, weewy bad? Think of *them*," she said, and turned to Georgia. "It'll be better in person. Trust me, this is the best way."

Georgia heard her mother's voice through the stuffing in her head.

"Georgia? Georgia, are you even listening?" Blythe hitched Rosie higher on her hip. "Georgia, honey, this is no time for whistling."

In the quiet of the house, Georgia's thoughts were loud and jangly. She decided to go through her suitcase one more time and make sure she had everything. She got up and turned her bedside lamp on low, and heaved the bag onto her bed. She unzipped it, took everything out. She counted her underwear and her socks, her T-shirts and shorts. She had the one nice yellow dress "for meeting the NASA people." Journal, sandals, sneakers.

There were lots of things she didn't have room for. Her boxed set of Chronicles of Narnia, her kaleidoscope. Lots of things she couldn't bring. Things and people and Freddy. She thought of Winslow, left behind, and Roly, choosing one brother over another. No wonder Roly'd left so fast. He probably couldn't stand it. If he'd had to think about it, he'd have gone crazy. Did Roly feel as though he'd left part of himself behind with Winslow?

She got out a piece of paper from her desk and penciled a line down the center.

At the top of one side, she wrote: *BaRB* (for Blythe and Rosie, Boat). Under that, she wrote *Mom, Rosie, See the World*. She wrote *NASA*. Then she erased it.

On the other side of the line she wrote: *NoB* (for No Boat). Under that she wrote *Dad, Maria, Freddy*. Then she wrote *Winslow. Lita. Patty van Winkle. School. Lyle*. These things and these people were all important. The NoB side was about an inch and a half longer than the BaRB side.

She would stay, then. The list was telling her not to

get on the boat with Blythe. She looked out the window at the night. So. Her choices could be measured, very simply, by the inch.

She looked at the list again. She didn't want to leave; she didn't. Except for one thing. She took her pencil and circled one word under the BaRB heading, around and around till the pencil mark shined: *Rosie*. It was not possible, after all, to measure her choices with a ruler.

If only she could talk to Maria. She could call her. Blythe wouldn't even know. She padded downstairs to the kitchen and called Maria's house. Someone picked up on the first ring.

"Hola."

"Lita?"

"Georgie, we've got to stop meeting like this," Lita said. A quiet, nighttime voice.

"Can I talk to Maria?"

"Not at one in the morning, you can't."

"I'm sorry."

"You okay, *mija*? Is your mama home?"

"Yes; I mean no. Yes, she's here."

"Okay, good. Why are you not sleeping?"

It was quiet on the phone.

"I'm—trying to figure everything out," Georgia said.

"Ah. I see." Georgia heard the quiet ember of Lita's

cigarette, pictured the thin stream of smoke. "Never gonna happen, *mija*."

Georgia twisted a button of her pajamas. "Why aren't *you* asleep?"

"Eh. Old ladies like me, we don't sleep much. In the night we see things . . ." Now Georgia pictured her nodding, gazing out the window at the moon.

"I just feel—I feel far away. I feel very far from myself." Georgia listened to Lita breathing.

"Sometimes," Lita said, "sometimes, *mija*, the inside and outside of ourselves—they don't match up. The outside is too big or too small. The inside rattles around, or presses like a flood, like fire. Or the inside is, as you say, very far away." There was an ashy sound, a small *clink* and slide of a saucer. "Part of my *self* I left in Oaxaca. But—and yet—that part, too, is inside me. In my heart. I am larger than my skin and bones. You know what I mean?"

Georgia nodded. Lita wasn't making a lot of sense. But her words made Georgia think of Freddy shedding his skin, and how she would find the dry husks in the sand. It was always hard to believe the bits and pieces of shed skin had ever held Freddy's body.

"I dream of Oaxaca . . ." Georgia heard the rasp of the lighter, the catch of the flame. "Oaxaca, even while I'm awake," Lita said. "But"—Georgia could picture the shrug of a shoulder, the casual hand, the cigarette between two fingers—"my world is here. The world is made. And it can be made again."

"Like Freddy?" Georgia stood a little straighter.

"Hmm?"

"Like how Freddy has a new skin under the old skin?"

"Okay, like Freddy."

"So I'm like Freddy."

"Sure, okay." Another drag on the cigarette.

The image of herself as a lizard seemed reasonable. Georgia liked it.

"Go to sleep now, *mija*. You can shed your skin in the morning, okay? Tomorrow you can make the world."

The kitchen was dark. The moonlight coming in the window cast squares of white on the linoleum like a big checkerboard. A game being played by huge forces—the moon and the night.

"She'll call you in the morning," Lita said. "Go to sleep."

"Early?"

"*Sí*, early."

"You'll tell her?"

"*Sí*, I'll tell her. Go to sleep now," Lita said, soft like a lullaby. "Go to sleep."

Georgia climbed back upstairs and went to her room. The suitcase was open on her bed, and she was too tired now to lift it. She left it where it was and went to Rosie.

Rosie was fast asleep on her back, her soft lips parted, her breaths deep and even. Georgia wished she could crawl into the crib beside her. She was so small and so sweet. Georgia put her hand on Rosie's warm tummy, and felt it rise and fall. She wanted to stay in Prospect Harbor, she knew that now, but—Rosie.

Rosie. She couldn't watch Blythe take Rosie away. Because she loved her so much, and because—she saw it now. Blythe wasn't . . . she didn't seem . . . safe.

So. She would go with Blythe in the morning. For Rosie's sake, she'd go.

Georgia slid the curtains back to let in the moonlight. Then she curled up on the fluffy rug beside the crib and fell asleep.

Chapter 28

Georgia remembered the long day yesterday, and the long night. She had talked with Lita—it seemed like a dream, but she remembered the whole thing, every word. She remembered opening the curtains and lying down in the moonlight. She opened her eyes. She was looking up at Rosie, whose face was pressed to the slats of her crib.

"Good morning." Georgia stood and lowered the rail and picked her up. "I got you," she whispered, as she always did.

"Ahgashoo," Rosie whispered.

"I got you," Georgia said again, in a regular voice.

"Ahgashoo," Rosie said, loud this time. Georgia laughed. "Yes, that's right, Rosie!" and Rosie laughed and kicked her little feet and held on tight to Georgia's pajama top.

She carried Rosie past her room, the suitcase still open on the bed. Clothes discarded like a skin.

She felt sad, and also not sad.

She walked down the stairs to the kitchen.

And she had an idea.

"Georgia—this is *bananas*. Don't be ridiculous." Blythe put down her coffee cup. "I'm her mother! I could never leave my baby!"

Quick anger flared. Georgia opened her mouth, closed it. Swallowed.

Blythe spooned applesauce into Rosie's mouth. "Good news, though; forget the bus to the other bus to the train, 'cause I've rented a car!"

"You left *me*." There. She said it. "You left me."

Blythe stared at her, her eyes wary, darting as if looking for a way out of a trap. Then she closed her eyes for a moment and waved the spoon, dismissive. Rosie fussed for more applesauce. "That was different. You weren't a little baby."

Georgia watched Blythe scrape the last of the applesauce from the dish and feed it to Rosie. *I was* your *baby.* But she didn't say it. It sounded—babyish. "I know what I need to know."

"What's that supposed to mean? You're a child."
She unfastened Rosie and lifted her from her high chair.

"I *know*."

"Georgia, stop it. This is my dream job!" Blythe
hitched Rosie higher on her hip. "I thought we were
alike, you and me. What about *your* dream of being an
astronaut?"

"I made it up."

"Why would you do that?" She jostled Rosie. "God,
you're heavy. Well, it doesn't matter. I once dreamed
of being a tollbooth attendant. Dreams change! Sometimes a dream is just a dream: nonsense in the night.
Now come on."

Georgia thought about the dream she'd had about
Rosie. The shards of shattered glass. She thought of
Lita's dreams, Oaxaca, and her words *the world is made*.

"Look, we *have* to get going if we're going to make
New Jersey by the time I have to turn the car in."

"What about Dad?"

"We'll swing by the house on our way—"

"He's at the plant, he's got a shift. It was on the
schedule—"

"We don't have time to go all the way to the plant,
the exact opposite direction—"

The phone buzzed.

"That's Maria. You said I could—"

"How was I supposed to know you'd oversleep?"

The dream came back into Georgia's mind, the terrible dream; she'd covered Rosie with her T-shirt. To protect her.

"Georgia, move it now. You're coming with me." The phone stopped buzzing. Blythe kept saying words, words, words. "I can't take this job if you don't come with me! What will I do with the baby? I need you, Georgia. Where's your sense of adventure?"

Georgia reached out her hands to Rosie, and Rosie leaned toward her. Off-balance, Blythe stumbled and Rosie fell into Georgia's arms.

Georgia bounced Rosie to adjust the solid weight of her. "I gave Freddy a better life," she said. "At least I tried!"

Blythe barked a laugh. "You left Freddy for your dad to take care of!"

"You left *me* for Dad to take care of!"

Everything went silent. Nothing and nobody moved, as if all the air went out of the room.

The phone chirped again and Georgia looked toward it. Blythe drew Georgia's face back with a finger on her cheek, and then tapped Georgia's forehead. "Rosie"—*tap*—"is not"—*tap*—"a lizard."

The phone stopped. Georgia thought of how well she'd done feeding Rosie and changing her diaper and putting her down to sleep, comforting her when she cried.

"I think I can do it." Georgia stood straight. She felt a little bit proud. She felt a little bit more certain than she had even a moment ago.

Blythe focused on a spot near where the ceiling met the wall, as if adding numbers on a board. Then she shook her head to clear whatever equation she'd figured.

"School will start soon and you won't have all this free time to watch her." Blythe put out her hands. "Give her to me. Go get your suitcase. Heidi's going to show up any minute." She glanced out the window. "She's giving us a ride to the Rent-A-Car."

"I would have lots of help." Georgia swayed, rocking Rosie gently side to side, and held on tight. She *would* have help. She knew she would. People had helped her before.

"Georgia, no. You're being childish and silly." But even at the same time Blythe said the words—*no— childish—silly*—her eyes grew keen and sharp.

Georgia pushed a little harder. "Just let me ask Dad what he thinks. I'll call Lyle. What time is it in in Arizona?" Rosie gripped the neck of Georgia's shirt.

A knot gathered between Blythe's brows. She was thinking. She was considering the idea. Wasn't she?

Georgia felt big forces on her side, almost as if it

hadn't been her idea at all, but the moon's in the night! It was just that big.

"We don't have time, Georgia. We have to get on that highway, or I'll be looking at a second-day rental on top of the drop-off fee!"

Blythe was talking about highways and money and hurry-hurry-up; Georgia was talking about right now and Prospect Harbor and the rest of her life. Georgia felt completely separate from Blythe, then, as if they were simply moving pieces on a game board, or acting out a play. Her breaths came deep and even. Rosie weighed nothing in her arms. What if she just—walked out the front door? What if she just—did it? What then?

"Georgia, let's go! You're making me frantic!"

"Mom, you don't have to worry." Georgia moved back a step, one step away from Blythe. "It's okay if you go." Was that what she meant?

"Georgia!" Blythe stomped her foot. "What are you saying?"

Georgia could hardly tell if she was actually doing what she *seemed* to be doing. Was she holding Rosie? Was she backing away from Blythe? It felt like moving through water, or mud. Even so, she could see the next step, the right step, on the path that led somewhere that wasn't a cruise ship with Blythe. "We'll be okay," Georgia said.

"Who's *we*?" Blythe spat out.

Rosie babbled and grabbed a little fistful of Georgia's hair. She said it again. "We'll be okay."

Blythe's face reddened right up to her blonde hair, her lips a thin, angry line. She threw her hands in the air. "This is nuts," she said to the ceiling. "This is the *height* of absurdity." Then she crossed her arms and glared. "It's done, Georgia. It's going to be *whacktastic*, you said it yourself."

Georgia shrank back, wrapped her arms tighter around Rosie. She felt Rosie's little hand patting her chest gently, and she looked down just as Rosie looked up and their eyes met. Rosie gurgled happily, as if she—a baby—knew everything there was to know, and even knowing everything, feared nothing. As if they were saying at the same time to each other the only word Rosie even knew—*I-got-you.*

"We'll be okay," Georgia said one more time.

"Yeah? Says *who*?"

Georgia swallowed hard. "Me."

"What?" said Blythe.

"Says me."

Then Georgia turned . . .

"Georgia? Georgia! Georgia, don't you walk away from me!"

Chapter 29

When you begin to cry, whistling is nearly impossible. It's very hard to maintain a pucker.

Georgia—whistling to be brave—yanked the door shut behind her and grabbed the umbrella stroller and—for once!—Rosie's legs went straight where the legs should go, and Georgia buckled her in and took off running. She didn't dare look back. What if Blythe was coming after them? What if she wasn't?

She ran as far as she was able. Then she walked fast and kept on walking all the way to the bay. She knew her dad would be at the plant, because she always knew where he would be. His schedule was right there on the fridge under the lobster magnet.

"Well, hello there, Georgie! To what do we at Harmon Lobster owe the pleasure?" Florence Deonn sat behind the reception desk and smiled her vermilion smile. She gave a tiny baby wave to Rosie. Rosie kick-kicked. Then Florence Deonn's smile dropped. "Oh my word. Did you walk all the way here?"

Georgia didn't want to cry. If she had to open her mouth, she'd cry; she knew she would.

Florence nodded. "Mmhmm," she said. "You have a seat right there." She pointed to the visitor's chair, which was overstuffed and loudly flowered and very comfortable.

A push against the edge of the desk sent Florence's wheeled chair across to a microphone. She flipped a switch and a loudspeaker carried the pleasant boom of her voice out over the facility floor. Georgia imagined all the workers perking up and being fortified just by hearing Florence, no matter what she might be saying. "*Stan*-ley Wea*thers*, *ple-ase* come to the office. *Staaan*-ley Weathers! *Off*ice, please." Florence made it sound like poetry. She clicked off the microphone, spun back to her desk, and looked at Georgia.

Florence had a very kind face, and right now it wore an expression of deep understanding. She was also a hugger, and Georgia knew from past experience at the annual Harmon Lobster company picnic that a hug from Florence Deonn was a wonderful thing. She knew, too, that if Florence came out from behind that desk and hugged her right now, then Georgia would start to bawl her head off and never stop.

"It's a hot one out there!" Florence said instead, as if it were perfectly normal to see Georgia at the plant and sitting there in the flowered chair and not saying a single word. She just plain couldn't speak. Florence didn't seem to mind.

"Nice and cool in here, though," Florence said. "I like to keep it that way. I like it so I can wear long sleeves and a *sweater* in here no matter the season."

Florence busied herself moving papers around her desk. "I do not enjoy an overwarm reception area." She shook her head. "No, I do not. A person has got to keep cool in hot times."

It didn't take her father long at all, and there he was in the doorway in his coveralls and steel-toed boots.

Georgia stood. Rosie babbled.

Stanley Weathers didn't say one word. He went to her in two strides and put his arms around her and held her tight so that her nose smooshed against his shirt front till she was able to turn her head to one side. He stank of the sea. Georgia didn't care. He felt very strong, and suddenly Georgia didn't, and that was okay.

Florence Deonn tugged a hankie from her cuff and dabbed her eyes. "I do *not* know what is going on, but whatever it is, baby, you go ahead and cry; your daddy's gonna hold you up." With that, Georgia sobbed in earnest. Rosemary let out several long, eardrum-piercing wails, and Florence blew her nose.

Over these noises of sadness and confusion and distress, Stanley Weathers finally spoke: "What is stronger than the human heart, which shatters and still lives?" Was it the clear, steady sound of his voice, or the words themselves, that shocked the others into silence? This was followed immediately by renewed crying and wailing and nose-blowing.

"Amen!" pronounced Florence.

"I saw it on a tea bag in the breakroom."

That only made everybody cry louder.

Chapter 30

Time slowed for a little while near the tail end of summer. School would start soon; Mr. and Mrs. Garcia would close up the Scamp and move back into the house; Lita would quit smoking again. The purple asters had begun to bloom. Georgia could smell the change of season this morning; her bedroom curtain fluttered with the push and pull of autumn on the way.

Georgia sprinkled some cockroaches into Freddy's tank. He gobbled them up, and when he was finished he stood there with his mouth wide open; it looked like he was smiling.

Georgia had an interesting, even jot-worthy, thought. In all that time she'd spent trying to give

Freddy a better life, maybe she was really figuring out how to make her own life better. She reached into the tank and lifted Freddy and held him in front of her, eye to eye. "Tell me, Freddy, are you a symbol or a metaphor?" She'd have to ask Maria. Either way, Freddy's life *was* better, and so was hers.

Georgia stroked Freddy's head and put him back in his tank. Freddy waved his foot and licked his eyeball. There was a postcard taped to the side of the tank now, with a picture of a red covered bridge. She didn't need to see the other side; she knew the words by heart.

As she went down the stairs she heard music playing, some laughter, and a bang of a pot or a pan.

She came to the kitchen, and there was Rosie in her high chair, pinching Oaty-O's off the tray and slipping them carefully between her lips. "Gee-gee!" Some Oaty-O's flew out of her mouth. Georgia went and kissed the top of Rosie's head and wiped her sticky hands with a cloth.

Lyle was there. He had on the GOOD-LOOKIN' IS COOKIN' apron. He'd quit his job—his heart wasn't in it, and he didn't want to travel—and decided to try to cobble something else together. So far he'd taught a minicourse at the Sardine School—"Lunch Bunch: Beyond PB&J." He'd applied to teach culinary arts part-time at the high

school. He had some leads on maybe doing some cater-
ing out of Georgia's dad's house, where there was more
counter space than the house on Belmont. And he was
teaching Stan how to cook.

"Maybe that could be the name of your new business," Georgia said. She hefted Rosie out of the high
chair. Rosie weighed a ton. Healthy as a horse, according to the well-visit nurse.

"What could?"

"'Good-Lookin' Cookin'.'" She settled Rosie on her
hip and pointed at Lyle.

They all studied Lyle's apron front, even Rosie. It
made a lot of sense.

Stan patted the front of the apron *he* was wearing.
"What about this one?" he said.

In the past month, Georgia and her dad had talked
more than they had in probably all of the two years
before. They talked about dreams and about Georgia
not really wanting to be an astronaut. They talked about
warm blood and cold hearts. They talked about all the
many comings and goings that happened in their lives.
"Real happiness lies in that which never comes nor
goes, but simply is," Stan had said over a soapy sink full
of dishes. He'd seen it on a tea bag.

"'Relish Today, Ketchup Tomorrow,'" Lyle read off

Stan's apron. "They're both good!" In his enthusiasm he knocked over the pepper grinder—"Oops!"—and sneezed.

"Bless you," Stan said.

"Shoo," Rosie said.

Georgia peered at the wall calendar. At the moment, Blythe would be, let's see, somewhere approaching the Bay of Fundy. Stan had written it all there in colored pencil, ocean blue, so that Georgia could be sure of Blythe's whereabouts every day. The Elegance Cruise Lines brochure with the route on the map was taped to the wall, and so was a postcard from Cape Liberty that pictured a ship on the front. With all the things on the wall, and the people and the noise and pots and pans, it was starting to feel like Maria's kitchen in here.

Georgia slung the ducky diaper bag over her shoulder and opened the door.

"Chicken fricassee for supper!" Georgia's dad called out.

"And blueberry cake!" hollered Lyle.

Outside she buckled Rosie into the stroller and paraded down the street and toward the green.

Passing the Voice of the Trumpet, she waved to Maria's brothers, who were shooting hoops and talking trash, she supposed.

"Nice one!" shouted Martin.

"Thanks!" hollered Miguel.

As she passed the Pet Stop, Patty van Winkle came bursting out the door—*jing-a-ling!*—wielding a bone-shaped biscuit. "Georgia, guess what!" She made smoochie noises at Rosie.

"What?"

"The tristate shortage of crickets is over!"

That was good news! But it was good to know Freddy could also thrive on cockroaches if there ever was another shortage of crickets.

Patty handed Rosie the dog biscuit. "What? I make them myself. They're one hundred percent fit for human consumption. Just rock-hard cookies, really. Excellent for teething." To prove her point, Patty pulled another one from her smock pocket and gnawed on it as she went back inside the shop.

Georgia pushed the stroller onward.

"There she is! There's my little sack of potatoes!" Florence Deonn stood up from the library bench as Georgia checked her watch: ten o'clock. Plenty of day ahead. Maybe they'd do some more work on the secret fort they were making among the lilacs alongside the Farleys' garage. Winslow had already brought some artwork to weave into the twigged walls—a photo of him and Roly with sparklers in their hands, and a post-card from Roly with a picture of a bike. And he'd even brought out Boat in a fishbowl for a visit.

Florence scooched and kissed the top of Rosie's head. "Are you ready for your auntie Florence?" She'd gone part-time at Harmon Lobster so she could take care of Rosie on a regular schedule, which was written on the calendar in vermilion red. The double doors of the library were opening. Georgia knelt and wiped some gooey dog biscuit from Rosie's chin.

"See you on the flip-flop," said Florence. She took the ducky diaper bag from Georgia and pushed the stroller up the ramp to story time.

Georgia waved and walked on.

Outside the post office, Maria was waiting. "Once the villain is vanquished," she said, "the story usually wraps up pretty quickly." She slammed shut the book she was reading. *Fabulous Fiction II: Even More Fabulous*.

"She isn't a villain."

"I'm not talking about Blythe. I'm talking about fabulous fiction."

Mr. Grigg switched the sign in the window: MAIL: YES, and they went inside.

Nothing, this time, from Blythe; there had been only

the one card in the month she'd been gone. But she'd called several times—from Newport and St. John, from Halifax, from Charlottetown. The passengers loved her singing, and she was keeping an eye out to make those NASA connections. She and Lyle were, as he put it, "navigating" their relationship. In fact, they were *all* of them navigating their relationships with Blythe; maybe they'd be navigating forever; maybe the sailing would never be smooth.

They pushed through the doors and out into the warmth of the day. Maria paged through the *Rare Reminder* as she walked. Suddenly, she gasped. "*¡Ay Dios mío!* They published it!" She jumped up and down, the newspaper crushed to her chest. "Look, look, look! I'm a published author!"

Georgia started jumping up and down along with her. "Let me *see* it!"

There, on page seven, in the Prospect Harbor Hometown Talent section, was a poem written by Maria, titled "Dumb Decision."

Maria recited the poem loud enough to draw a small crowd.

"'KA-POW!
Is the sound of

Someone's dumb decision
Spectacularly going up
In smoke.'"

The crowd—Ms. Bennett and her dog, Booksie—clapped and barked.

"It's really good!" Georgia said.

"I know!" Maria plopped down happily on the curb. "Five lines and twenty-two syllables make a cinquain. It's a very challenging form."

Ms. Bennett and Booksie went on their way, and Georgia sat down beside Maria.

"Maybe I ought to forget about being a writer of romance or suspense," Maria said. "I can't think how to end *The Dragon in the Glass Castle* except for happily ever after."

"What's wrong with that?"

"Georgia, above all else a writer must write *truth*."

"Well—happily ever after might be true," Georgia said.

Maria thought about it. "I think I'll go with happily. Happily ever after's a stretch. Just—happily. That's good enough."

Georgia thought about her world—the calm of Prospect Harbor, the rough waters out beyond the harbor's hug, the parade of people and pets and family and friends, all the reasons for love in her heart. "It's good enough," she said. "It's whacktastic, even."

Along with the *Rare Reminder*, Georgia and Maria had received postcards addressed in their own hands— their third, each, from Roland Park. They checked the postmark: Boston. They hoped he would provide an address one of these times before the cards ran out.

Maria poked up her glasses and read her card, which pictured a seagull, and smiled. "Innnnnteresting." She tucked the postcard into her flowered tote.

Georgia's card pictured a birch tree and a chicka-dee. She turned it over in her hands; she didn't need to read the words. They'd be the same words he'd scrawled on the ones with the bike and the gull and the autumn-colored trees; the one with the red covered bridge. But she read it anyway.

Keep on Truckin'.

She hoped for more, but for now, it was enough.

ACKNOWLEDGMENTS

I had a lot of help writing this book! Special thanks first to Francesca and Georgia and the real Freddy, who is living his best life with his girlfriend Whitney, but that's a different story.

Innumerable thanks to Sylvie and Paula and Krista and Hilary and all the supportive, creative people on the S&S team, who make everything so much better, and to Charles Santoso for illustrating Freddy as the cover-boy he deserves to be. Sarah Sentilles and the Word Cave April 2020 supported me through a pandemical final revision. Thanks to the Butterfly Sisters for steady companionship and (unsteady?) laughs and to Jeannie for all the love and puppy pictures.

Finally, always and ever, 🙏 and 🖤 to the best group text: la fam 😎 😎 😎 ✌️ ✌️ ✌️